MY HUSBAND'S FIANCÉE

WENDY OWENS

ORANGEWILLOW PUBLISHING

Copyright © 2021 by Wendy Owens

All rights reserved.

No part of this book may be reproduced in any form or by any electronic or mechanical means, including information storage and retrieval systems, without written permission from the author, except for the use of brief quotations in a book review.

❀ Created with Vellum

For my Family, Josh, Zoe, Brayden and Penny - When I don't want to strangle you all I am thankful you're my crew. I love each and everyone of you to bits and tiny little pieces.

NEWSLETTER

Do you want to make sure you don't miss any upcoming releases or giveaways? Be sure to sign up for my newsletter at http://signup.wendyowensbooks.com/

PROLOGUE
TUESDAY, FEBRUARY 6TH, 2018

I'd awoken that morning with a bad feeling. I'd had a bad feeling the day our child died. I'd had a bad feeling the day I'd discovered my husband was having an affair. I was a bit of an expert on bad feelings.

When I'd heard the sound of multiple car doors slamming shut in front of our house later that day, I'd known it wasn't going to be good before I ever saw the blue and red strobes. *They're back,* I'd thought to myself in a panic before I cried out for my husband.

"Nathan." His name hung in the air as I rushed from our master suite and bounded down the steps, darting through the vast entry into the wood-paneled hall that led to our kitchen. "Nathan!" I shouted. The sound of my heart pumping pounded in my ears.

When I entered the kitchen and saw no sign of him, my stomach twisted and tied itself into knots. I knew the knock would be coming in a matter of moments. I couldn't answer the door. It was too frightening to think that if the police took Nathan, I may not get him back.

"Nathan!" I shouted again, and my voice cracked with desperation. I heard shoes beating against the wooden floors, and relief washed over me when I saw him emerge from the opening on the far side of the room.

"Lizzy, what's wrong?" Nathan peered at me with concerned eyes.

"Where were you? I-I couldn't find you," I stammered, doing my best not to let my growing fear of what was coming overwhelm me.

He gripped my upper arms with his strong hands, and as if by instinct, I started to calm. "I was in my study." I should have guessed where to find him. Nathan spent most of his time there since—the murder. I watched him as his head jerked toward the front of the house, the clatter outside drawing his attention. The flashing of the blue and red lights had managed to find their way through the glass of our front door, danced across the entry and down the long hall, and reflected off the French doors that led out to our courtyard. I thought of what the courtyard must have looked like with the shimmering police lights breaking through. The place where we'd shared picnics. The place Nathan had kissed my stomach as we dreamed of what our lives would be like once our family was complete.

I held my breath and watched as his mouth opened, waiting for him to speak, but nothing came out. He looked back at me when the chimes of the entry bell filled our home.

"It's them," I whispered. "What are we going to do?" I felt my throat as it closed around my words. He released his grip on me, and I followed closely as he stepped into the hall and started to inch his way toward the entry.

I had the instinct to run, to pull on his arm and beg him to sprint out the back door and not stop until we'd left this horrible nightmare far behind us. I knew, though, there was nowhere to go.

Nathan reached out and grasped my hand as we both came to stand in the center of the entryway. The twenty-four-foot ceilings of openness and the antique chandelier that hung in it had felt so grand and massive when we'd first purchased the home. Now, with the silhouette of the officers looming on the other side of the front door, I couldn't help but feel trapped.

The bell chimed again, and as it rang throughout our home, my chest rattled. The detective announced himself loudly from outside. Nathan moved toward the door, and I reached out and swiped at the air as I tried to grab him.

"We could run," I blurted out in a hushed tone, surprised I'd actually suggested the insane idea. He would know as much as I did that it was too late to run.

"What?" He stopped and turned to look at me with a confused expression on his face.

"I can't lose you," I replied, my voice betraying just how scared I was.

"I promise, you're never going to lose me," he assured me, but I couldn't break my eyes away from the figures on the other side of the glass. "Lizzy, do you hear me?"

"You can't say that," I answered at last.

"I can, and I did," he replied. "Now I need to answer the door, okay?"

I shook my head wildly. "I have a bad feeling. Please, trust me." He couldn't have known that I knew exactly what I was talking about. I'd never shared with him that I'd had the same feeling so many times before. If we opened that door, I knew our lives would never be the same.

Closing the gap between us one last time, he reached out and touched my cheek. "Babe, take a deep breath. I didn't do this, do you understand me?" I nodded. "That's why everything is going to be okay. I almost destroyed our lives once. I won't ever do anything to hurt you again. You believe me, don't you?"

I nodded again. And I did believe that he didn't want to hurt me. The affair was a blip in the ten years we'd been together, a weakness I could see he regretted. The problem was that I wasn't sure if he had any power to stop what would be set into motion once he opened that door.

"I have to answer them, though," he added. "Or they'll think we're trying to hide something."

Nathan hadn't known I was hiding something. A secret I could never tell him. I learned about the affair before he'd ever told me. He wouldn't have understood. I could see how sorry he was for what he'd done, and I didn't want to undo all the progress we'd made. If I told him I had been following him, that I'd been lying to him for months, he wouldn't understand.

He paused and studied me for a moment. I could see his eyes were swollen and red. I wondered if he'd been crying over her again. The other woman. The woman who had tried to steal him away. I knew his tears were because he was a good man, and any good man would be troubled when someone's life had been snuffed out as hers had been. It didn't mean he loved her, only that he cared about her in some small way.

He offered me a half-smile. "It's going to be fine," he said one last time. Turning, he took several long strides, leaving me standing alone behind the marble-topped circular entry table. I braced myself when he stopped at the door and prepared for our lives to be shattered.

I nodded, sniffed, and dried my cheeks. I tried to hide any evidence of my distress, then held my breath as Nathan looked over his shoulder one last time and pulled the door open.

My mind started to race. I wondered if they would put him in handcuffs this time. They hadn't last time, only asked him to come with them to answer questions. It had only been a month, so I hadn't expected to see them again so soon. They'd asked me questions the same day, but I'd been able to stay in our home while they questioned me. I'd sat on our brown leather sofa in our sitting room as they asked me about Nathan and his whereabouts on the night of Alison's untimely death. They'd asked if I had known that Nathan was having an affair, to which, of course, I lied in my response.

They didn't ask me if I had killed Alison. Why would they? After all, I didn't kill her, despite contemplating it on several occasions. I wasn't insane, but I was also only human. During the nights he'd spent with her, it was only natural my mind would go to dark places. At least, that was what I had told myself.

The problem was if it wasn't me, then, of course, it

had crossed my mind that Nathan could have been responsible. I refused to let the idea linger, though. Despite our attempts to feign a picturesque life that was the envy of our friends, we had problems. Problems we'd become very skilled at hiding from the outside world. Every marriage had issues, though, and I'd told myself, though our marriage wasn't perfect, I would have known if my husband were a killer.

I'd gone over the night of Alison's death so many times in my head. There was a chance it was all a coincidence. Supposedly, the woman had walked in on a home intruder, though this theory seemed quite improbable. I'd also come to consider that perhaps Nathan wasn't the only married man she'd seduced. Although I had seen no evidence of such a relationship in my surveillance of her, it wasn't out of the realm of possibilities.

Surveillance. I could see how, from an outside perspective, it didn't look good that I'd been keeping tabs on Nathan and his new girlfriend. If I thought I had any information that could help exonerate Nathan, I'd undoubtedly offer it up. But in the absence of such information, I'd decided it best I remained silent about my activities surrounding the recently deceased woman.

I hadn't been a good wife. At least that was how I explained Nathan's betrayal in my mind. After we'd lost our son, I'd been cold and distant. No matter how much he tried to connect with me, I had been determined to keep Nathan at arm's length. When I'd found out about the affair, I made the decision that things had to change. I would have to own the part I had played in the failure of our marriage by pushing Nathan away. I would be a better wife. I would be the wife he'd fallen in love with all those years ago.

I looked down to see I had started gripping the edge of the table in front of me at some point because my knuckles were white. To the right of the front door were the stairs that led up to the master suite and to the left was the opening that led to the formal sitting room. I considered taking flight to one or the other to hide and wait for news of the inevitable. That was when my eyes landed on the face of the police detective.

He was staring past Nathan and directly at me. The ground beneath me felt like it was shifting like the waves under my stepfather's boat. I'd grown up in Rockport, Massachusetts, and after my dad walked out on our family, my mom had made her way through countless men, looking for one to support us. My stepdad, Phil, owned a fishing boat company, and while he wasn't wealthy in the standards of the circles Nathan had brought me into, he had been exactly what my mother was looking for. I hadn't realized how much I had needed him as well. He was the shining light of my childhood. Being out on the water with him, with the boat rocking, somehow felt calmer to me than the storms inside my home with my mother. I stiffened as I grasped onto a memory of Phil telling me how brave I was when a storm rolled in on us. *Everything is going to be okay,* I told myself, just as he had.

I attempted to push aside the white noise that had filled my head, focusing on Nathan as he exchanged words with the detective. They both repeatedly looked in my direction. "My wife?" Nathan barked. "No, you . . ." His voice trailed off, and my temples started to throb. He was quiet now, talking to the detective in an almost whisper.

Me? What could they possibly have to discuss with me? I'd gone over all of the things that could have connected me to that night. I'd been careful. I'd thought everything out. There was no way they could be looking at me. Nathan studied a piece of paper the detective had handed him. He then stepped to one side, allowing the officers entrance into our home.

As if it were a choreographed dance, the detective moved closer to me, barking instructions to the other officers. They dispersed into the sitting room and started pulling open drawers and rifling through the contents. One tossed a notebook into an empty box while another opened up a plastic bag and proceeded to place a hairbrush in it that had fallen out of my purse earlier that day.

"Excuse me." The words croaked out of my throat, but nobody even looked at me. "Excuse me," I said again, louder. *You are brave.* "What are you doing?" I pushed myself fully upright. "You can't do this!"

My eyes darted to Nathan as he moved to lean against the railing at the bottom of the stairs. He wasn't speaking, and his shoulders slumped into a deflated stance. He just kept staring at that damn piece of paper the detective had given him.

"Honey!" I exclaimed. "They're taking our things. They can't do that."

My Husband's Fiancée 9

He licked his lips and, without looking at me, replied. "This search warrant says that they can."

Search warrant. I silently repeated the words to myself in my head. They had to have found something to obtain a search warrant. Had I not been as cautious as I'd thought?

"Why are they here?" I asked him, but he didn't raise his gaze to meet mine. My head started to bob when I watched two officers move in behind Nathan and begin to scale the stairs.

"Where are they going? Are they going into our bedroom?" I cried, recoiling into myself from the violation. "I don't give them permission to do that."

"Mrs. Foster," the detective said as he crossed the room, cutting the space between us in half. "As I was telling your husband, I have no wish to embarrass you in front of your neighbors."

"My neighbors?" I spat. "Why would I be embarrassed?"

"If you can agree to come quietly, we don't have to make a scene."

The pain in my temples exploded into a crippling throbbing as darkness crept into the corners of my vision. I stared at the detective's face. They weren't here for my husband. They were here for me. "I'm sorry, but what exactly are you saying?" My stomach fluttered as a wave of worry rushed through me.

"We need you to come to the precinct with us," he continued. He was a tall and wiry man. The ebony skin on his forehead glistened from the light of the chandelier overhead. I remembered when we'd first met and how I'd thought he had kind eyes. They still had that kindness, but something else was in them now. Suspicion? No, contempt.

I looked at Nathan, who was silently watching my interaction with the detective. Why hadn't he said anything? Why hadn't he come to my defense? "No, that doesn't make any sense. I . . ." A couple of the officers that had been riffling through our belongings started watching the scene unfold. I took a deep breath and began again. "I don't understand. Why do I have to go with you?"

"It would be better if we discussed this at the precinct," the detective stated, his voice so calm it made me think perhaps I'd misread the entire situation. "I've told your husband he can go ahead and contact your lawyer while we're on the way."

"Lawyer," I whispered as my head started to spin. No, I hadn't misread the situation at all. I sucked in a deep breath and strode past the detective and right up to my husband. Nathan flicked his eyes in my direction momentarily before pulling out his phone and scrolling through the contacts. "What's going on?" I asked him, my tone firm.

"You should go with them, Liz," he said as he found the number for Larry Putnam, our family attorney.

"What do they want?" I asked as my bottom lip started to shake.

"You heard the detective. They need to clear some things up with you," Nathan stated, his voice cold.

"What did you say to them?" I asked as I tried desperately to sort through the confusion in my head.

"Excuse me?" He gasped.

"You had to have said something. Why else would they want to talk to me? When they took you in before, did you say something about me? Is that why they're here?" I growled.

"Do you hear yourself?" Nathan asked.

"Go ahead, tell me how crazy I sound. We both know how you love to pull the crazy card on me," I snapped, the familiar pang of betrayal creeping in. He'd promised he would never hurt me again, but here we were, at the same place we always seemed to end up.

"Liz, stop," he said.

"Cheating on me wasn't enough? You have to get me twisted up in all of this too?"

His eyes widened, and his nostrils flared. That only happened when he was furious. "Don't," he warned firmly as he shook his head.

"Don't what? I didn't do a damn thing, and you know it."

He waved the piece of paper he had been holding in the air. "Did you hide cameras in her house?" His voice trembled when he asked the question.

"Her who?" The words tumbled out of my mouth as I tried to think of how they could know about the cameras. I thought I'd been so careful. I'd removed them and disposed of them. How could they possibly know about them?

He rolled his eyes. "You know damn well I'm talking about Alison. You put fucking cameras in her house?"

"What?" I feigned innocence and shock at his question. "I have no idea what you're talking about."

"Don't lie to me, Liz," he said.

"I—" I considered lying again, but it was suddenly apparent to me that I'd missed a detail somewhere. If they had a search warrant, they'd most certainly find everything I had hidden up in the attic. Lying at this point would only make me appear guilty.

"What did you do?" Nathan asked.

"Nothing, I swear," I pleaded as I reached out for his arm, but he pulled away.

Nathan never shouted. I could recall maybe five times in our marriage when he'd even slightly raised his voice. Everything felt surreal as I watched him yell and clench his fists in anger. "I can't believe you could do such a thing!"

He wasn't talking about the cameras anymore. I could see in his anger that he was talking about Alison's murder. He thought I killed her. "I didn't!" I hissed.

"They can't just make this shit up, Liz. You acted like you had no idea about the affair, but that was a lie. What else have you been lying about?" he asked, staring at me with disdain.

"How dare you?" He'd been the one having an affair, and he was going to stand there and judge me. He was the one who had jeopardized everything we'd built together.

"Seriously?" Nathan questioned. I felt the detective watching the entire interaction. "Jesus, Liz, it's like I don't even know who you are."

"Screw you, Nathan," I spat. "Where do you get off acting so high and mighty? She was pregnant, for Christ's sake."

Nathan dropped the paper and shifted his stance, pressing his back into the railing to create as much distance between us as possible. His face twisted into an expression I'd never seen on him, and it frightened me. He swallowed hard. "How did you know she was pregnant?" he whispered.

"What?" I asked, regretting the revelation. I shook my head. "You must have told me." But he hadn't told me. I'd found out about her pregnancy on my own just as I'd found out about the affair on my own.

Nathan's head dropped. "You shouldn't say anything else, Liz."

"What are you talking about? I didn't do anything," I insisted again.

Without warning, the detective was practically on top of me. I felt his hand as it gripped my arm. "Elizabeth Foster, you have the right to remain silent."

As he continued to read me my rights, I tried to pull away from him unsuccessfully. "I don't know then. I must have heard it on the news."

"That information had not been made public, Mrs. Foster," the detective informed me.

"Liz, don't say anything else until Larry gets there," Nathan interjected.

"You must have told me," I said to Nathan again as the detective tightened his grip and nudged me toward the door.

"Nathan!" I called out his name, fighting against the detective as he dragged me behind him.

The neighbors had already gathered. I felt their eyes burning into my flesh, but I didn't care. The detective lowered my head into the back seat of the vehicle. My bad feelings were never wrong.

∼

1

SATURDAY, JANUARY 5TH, 2019

PRESENT DAY

Three hundred thirty-three days. That was how long it had been since the night I was arrested. The trial prep lasted five months, while the trial itself only lasted three days. The jury took three hours to decide I was guilty. If you were accused of first-degree murder in Massachusetts, you were detained until trial most of the time. Despite my attorney's assurances I would be the exception, I quickly discovered he was incorrect. Larry had misjudged many aspects of my defense, which led to me choosing to dismiss him after the verdict and seek new counsel for my appeal.

The sea-foam green and cream walls of the MCI Farmington correctional facility had become my home. My sentence was life, and unless, by some miracle, I won my appeal, the four bunks inside my cell would be what I saw every night when I laid my head down to sleep. I'd been scared when I first arrived, but I was also determined not to show it. I hadn't been born rich, and my mother told me that was a blessing the night they processed me. She explained that I didn't ooze wealth, but if I had, many of the women would hate me where I was headed. She meant it as a comfort in her mind, but it only made me question things about myself, like most things with my mother. What did people see when they looked at me? Did they see a killer? What had people in Nathan's world seen when they looked at me if they didn't see a woman of wealth and stature? My mother's words only served to make me feel like an imposter, no matter what world I'd found myself in.

Nathan had never had to struggle. His mother was the lifelong mistress of a well-known businessman in Boston, and while Nathan was never given his father's last name, whispers of who his father was had opened doors for him his entire life. Our home had been primarily paid for by a generous gift from his father with the understanding we were never to make it public. It was a relationship Nathan didn't like to discuss and was determined not to repeat with his child.

These connections influenced his social circles in college, which led to future business relationships and ultimately his position managing one of the more considerable hedge funds for the firm he worked at. Nathan had once told me he never imagined becoming a hedge fund manager when he enrolled in college. Secretly, he'd always dreamed of making furniture. I remembered how surprised I had been when he revealed this to me. One of his friend's fathers had been a woodworker growing up, and he had always marveled at what he could make with his hands. He'd confessed to me that creating something useful from nothing always felt more inspiring than making rich men richer. One of Nathan's weaknesses, though, was his father and pleasing him. For a man we rarely saw or spoke to, he had an immense amount of influence over our lives.

I supposed he was a big part of why our lives always looked so perfect from the outside. A part of me hated it. I hated the role I had to play as the perfect wife and even better hostess. We would welcome people into our home who were foaming at the mouth for any piece of gossip they could use to cut someone else down. It was pretty tiring at times, but it was a part of the life I'd accepted that came along with Nathan. I'd always preferred the outliers, the strange ones in our social circles, the outcasts as they were viewed. I guess, in a way, I'd always thought of Nathan and myself as secret outcasts. We might have played our roles, but we were always longing to be who we were underneath. In a perfect world, Nathan would spend his days dreaming up and constructing furniture while I would write. I'd gone to school for journalism, but these days, the industry felt like it was dying a slow death. A secret that only Nathan knew was that I wanted to be a novelist. More specifically, a crime writer, though my penchant for dark criminal fantasies had likely contributed to my circumstances of being surrounded by iron bars.

The people I'd met since my incarceration were different from anyone I'd known. I couldn't imagine a single one of them pretending to be anyone else. I'd found that quality admirable. My bunkmate, Ruby Miller, had what another prisoner informed me was referred to as meth mouth. Past her chapped and cracked lips was a collection of decaying broken teeth and infected gums—a souvenir from her lifelong battle with addiction. But Ruby's teeth were not what I would say was the most memorable thing about her. Her crude sense of humor often left me in tears, but the thing that surprised me the most was her fierce loyalty. I had done nothing to earn it, but once she considered me a friend, it was mine.

Another inmate I'd befriended was Marla. She had one leg noticeably longer than the other, a full head of frizzy brown curls I imagined might look quite lovely with some product, and broad shoulders with matching hips. She once told me her mother named her after Marla Maples because she wanted her to have that kind of fairy-tale life. It surprised me when I realized she wasn't joking. I'm not sure I would have made it past the first week in this place if Marla hadn't taken a liking to me. For the life of me, I couldn't figure out why she liked me until Ruby explained Marla was impressed that I wasn't willing to lie down and take that my husband was cheating on me. I'd thought it best not to tell her I was innocent of the murder.

People in here did what Marla told them to. I didn't know what Marla did to command their respect, but it was clear nobody wanted to get on her bad side. I was relieved I'd found myself in her good graces.

One thing I'd found challenging to adjust to were the showers. The community bathrooms had individual stalls and open room showers. I was focused on getting in and out of the shower as quickly as possible, surprising even myself at how uncomfortable I was being naked in front of the other women.

None of the women in prison wanted to be there, and every one of them had their own story about what was waiting for them on the outside. Sometimes when I heard about the mothers missing their children, I found myself thinking of how little I had out in the world. If I ever managed to get out, nothing would be waiting for me. That thought didn't change how much I hated being here.

I'd lost at least ten pounds since my initial incarceration. Inmates did most of the cleaning around the prison, and after Ruby told me about the maggots she'd found in the meat grinder on her shift, I'd become a vegetarian.

The worst for me, though, weren't the showers or the food. It had to be the loneliness. It was incredible how much you could fill your time on the outside. When you take the busy work of day-to-day living away, a handful of friends couldn't quench that ache you had for connection. The days in prison were long, and I'd eagerly awaited my appeal.

When I walked into the visitor's lounge, I wasn't sure who was there to greet me. I was allowed eight names on my list of visitors. When I'd made the list, I was unaware that my husband was a bastard, so of course, he topped my list. There was my mother, sister, best friend from college, as well as a couple of neighbors I'd thought were probably as close to friends as I had in my life with Nathan. That was it. I couldn't even come up with eight names for my list. It had become just one more realization of how pitiful my life was.

If someone not on our list requested a visit, we were given their name and a note next to the request, explaining the purpose of their visit. Next to the visitor's name on that day was a note that read legal documents. In the commonwealth of Massachusetts, any inmate convicted of first-degree murder was automatically granted an appeal. Though I had not recognized the name, I assumed the visit was someone from my new lawyer's office based on the note.

I scanned the room as the guard escorted me inside. A woman smiled and waved as if she recognized me, which wasn't surprising since my face had been all over television for the past year. Her tailored clothes and pristine hair and makeup made me feel self-conscious of my new unkempt appearance. I glanced down at my gray scrubs before crossing the room and standing in front of the table.

"Are you here for Elizabeth Foster?" I asked.

She nodded and offered me a smile. "I am, hello." I quickly sat down across from her, knowing that the guards did not like it when inmates were not seated. The woman had shiny brown hair wrapped up into a tight twist on the back of her head. Her eyes were dark brown, and from the perfect symmetry of her eyebrows to the flawless application of her makeup, it was clear she took pride in her appearance. She stared at me from behind her tiny nose that turned up slightly at the end. I felt my stomach twist when I thought I might have spied a look of pity from her.

The woman opened her mouth to speak again, but this time, she hesitated.

"You have papers for me or something?" I finally asked in an irritated tone.

Chapter 1

She swallowed hard, pushing aside any nerves that might have been rattling her. "My name is Dr. Evelyn Powell."

Doctor? Had something changed with the plans on my appeal? No way was my lawyer thinking of going the insanity route. I'd made it quite clear I would never confess to a crime I didn't commit, even if it would have landed me in a psych hospital rather than here. I narrowed my eyes, making my instant disapproval evident.

"Thank you so much for agreeing to see me," she quickly continued.

"I didn't know who you were when I agreed."

"Oh." She breathed a disappointed breath.

I shook my head. "I haven't changed my mind. I refuse to plead insanity when I didn't do this. If your boss thinks you're going to come down here and convince me of that, she won't like what I have to say to her." I had changed lawyers after my initial conviction. Everyone I knew, except Nathan, said it was a mistake to stick with Larry from the start. But I trusted Nathan. At least at that point, I still did. The problem was, my mother was paying for my new legal defense, and her pockets were not as deep as my husband's had been, so my options this time around were limited.

"No," the doctor interjected. "I think there's been some sort of misunderstanding."

"What sort of misunderstanding? I said I'm not crazy."

"I'm not here for your case," she answered.

I shook my head, confused, and pushed away from

the table slightly. "I was told your visit was about getting me to sign some legal paperwork."

She looked worried. I noticed her hand trembling as she reached for an envelope that was tucked at her side.

"Who are you?" I asked pointedly, realizing she wasn't who I'd assumed.

She bit at her upper lip before straightening her back and lifting her chin as if defiantly refusing to let herself give in to her own fear. "As I said, my name is Dr. Evelyn Powell, and I'm . . ." She hesitated for only a moment. "Nathan's fiancée."

The words didn't make sense to me at first. "Nathan, who?" I asked, certain that she couldn't be talking about my Nathan.

She leaned a little closer and lowered her voice to a whisper. "Nathan Foster, your husband. I mean ex . . . I —" She stammered. He wasn't my ex anything. Nathan was still technically my husband.

I felt like I'd been punched in the gut. I'd had a lot of time to think about it since being locked away in this place. The only viable answer was that not only had Nathan cheated on me but he had also succeeded in framing me for the murder of his mistress. It seemed unimaginable, but apparently, he'd decided to twist the knife by sending in his latest conquest to talk to me.

"Excuse me?" I finally choked out, unable to hide my surprise.

"I know. I'm sure this comes as quite a shock, but please hear me out," Evelyn pleaded. "Nathan would kill me if he knew I was here."

"He doesn't know?" I laughed as I asked the question.

Perhaps I'd been mistaken. "Oh, you have no idea how right you are."

"Please, if you'll just let me explain," she begged.

"I don't have to fucking do anything you ask," I hissed. Before my time in prison, I hadn't had a very sharp tongue besides when I drank, but something about being in this place with these women felt empowering. The use of profanity had grown on me.

She swallowed a huge gulp of air and slumped back into her chair. For the first time, I noticed a look of familiar desperation on her face.

I'd started to stand but sat back down. "Why are you here?" I asked, confident I would likely regret the question.

"Really?" she asked, suddenly wide-eyed. "You'll listen?"

"You have two minutes," I told her. The truth was, the people I knew from my life before this place didn't visit very often. I was entitled to five visits per week, but I was lucky to get one. The thing I never knew about prison was how much boredom could get to a person. I needed something to engage my mind in. Anything not to think about the disaster my life had turned into. Though I hated to admit it, my curiosity was also stoked.

"Umm, well, as I said . . ." She bobbed her head cautiously. "Nathan has no idea I'm here. I knew if I didn't help him with this next step, it might never happen."

"Next step?" The words caught in my throat as if a chunk of apple had lodged itself there.

She exhaled, placed the envelope in front of her, and then folded her arms on top of it. "I want you to know that when I started to talk to Nathan, never in a million years did I imagine I would fall for him. It all happened so quickly."

"When you met him?"

She nodded. "It was in a grief group."

I laughed. The idea of Nathan attending a grief group when he was the one who was responsible for everything was an absolute joke.

Evelyn pushed on despite my flippant attitude. "I wanted to help him. I had no idea I would develop feelings for him."

"Yeah, you said that." I couldn't blame her. The truth was that Nathan and I had gotten engaged after only dating for three months. We were both getting ready to graduate from college and had gotten caught up in the excitement of our lives finally starting. He was easy to fall for. "I don't give a shit about you or your feelings for Nathan."

"Of course. You have to believe me, though. He carries so much guilt about his contributions to what—well, what put you here," she continued.

"He should!" I scoffed at the ridiculousness of her statement. "He's one hundred percent responsible for my being here."

"I think that's why he can't bring himself to ask you for the divorce," she said.

It felt as if I were a balloon, and all the air had deflated from me. "He doesn't need to ask me for one," I snapped, annoyed he had already seemed to move on with his life while I was stuck in this place. "All he has to do is file it with his lawyer, and they'll take care of it. I'm sure Larry has told him how it works. Jesus, he works quickly, doesn't he? It hasn't even been a year since my arrest."

If I was being honest, part of me had expected the divorce papers as soon as the verdict came back. I guess I'd resigned myself to the idea that Nathan had decided we would be stuck together. Forever. Each of us paying for the other's sins until we died. After all, I'd driven him to the affair. And who knows, if he hadn't stumbled across my plans to kill Alison, maybe he would have never had the idea, and the girl would still be alive. Neither of us was innocent in this.

"But that's just it. He won't," she added.

I was intrigued. "Won't what?"

"He says he can't bring himself to do that to you, at least not yet."

"Not yet?" I rolled my eyes as I repeated the words. "I'm sitting in prison with a life sentence for something I didn't do. I think it's pretty clear that Nathan doesn't give a shit about what he does to me."

"After everything he's told me about you, I told him you were strong enough to handle it." Did he speak about me to her? Did he make me out to be a psychopath? Was he the victim in his story?

I ground my teeth together. Not only did he frame me for the murder but now he also seemed to have trapped this poor woman with his manipulative lies.

I sighed. "Why would you want to marry a man who won't even ask his wife for a divorce?"

"Don't you see?" A smile pulled at the corners of her mouth. "That shows how selfless he is. He denies himself happiness because he had an affair, a moment of weakness. He thinks he doesn't deserve to be happy ever again because of that."

"A moment of weakness? Jesus, didn't you say you're supposed to be some sort of doctor?"

"I'm a therapist," she replied firmly, and I could tell I'd offended her.

"Look, I'm doing you a favor by telling you this. He's not the man you think he is. It's not just that he lies and cheats. He will do whatever it takes to save his own ass, and I mean anything. Mark my words; he won't hesitate to do to you what he did to me," I warned.

"I understand how hard this must be for you," she continued.

"Are you fucking kidding me? You're a therapist?" I repeated, and she nodded. "Well, you must be shit at your job if you couldn't even tell that the man you love is a fucking murderer."

She brushed her eyebrows with her fingertips as she considered my question for a moment. "I'm sorry, I didn't come here to upset you."

I scoffed. "Well, you fucking failed at that, didn't you?"

"This was a mistake," she muttered.

"No, you're about to make the biggest mistake of your life. I did not murder that woman."

"Look, I'm sorry this happened to you, but—"

"No, you're not hearing what I'm saying. If I didn't do it, there's only one person left who did."

"What?"

"Nathan was the only other one with motive and

opportunity," I replied, noticing a little fear behind her eyes that had not been there before.

"No, you're wrong," she insisted.

I pushed back off the table and crossed my arms in frustration. How could I make this woman see what a cunning narcissistic asshole that man was when I couldn't see it myself until it was too late?

That was precisely why I'd found myself behind bars. I figured out who Nathan really was when it was too late, and nobody was ever going to believe me now. The case against me was practically wrapped up with a bow on it. When all the pieces fell into place, the police quit digging, but there had to be something. Some piece of evidence that would link Nathan to the crime. He had forgotten something like I had. If I could make this woman see exactly who Nathan was, maybe she would help me uncover the missing piece of evidence that could set this right.

Evelyn's shoulders slumped in defeat but quickly perked up when I said, "I'll make you a deal."

"A deal?" She hesitated with a hopeful look on her face.

"You agree to keep coming here, and let me tell you my side of the story, and if at the end of it you still want to marry that piece of—" I stopped myself. "Nathan, I'll sign the papers."

"Are you serious?"

I nodded. "Yes, but I'm not signing anything until you've heard it all."

She considered the offer for a moment. If I was sincere, I was more concerned about saving my ass, but perhaps in the process, I could also be Evelyn's salvation by helping her see the truth before she made the same mistakes I did.

"Nathan can't find out," she said.

"Who's going to tell him?" I laughed.

She looked around the room as if concerned she was suddenly being watched and bit her bottom lip apprehensively before finally agreeing. "Okay, I'll do it."

"Great. I'll see you tomorrow?"

"I can't get away again until next week," she replied.

"Then next week it is." I nodded as I stood and walked toward the guard standing near the door that led back toward the cell block. Hope started to grow in the pit of my stomach.

∼

2

I heard movement in the water nearby, but I didn't stir. The water around me was still, and with a pool noodle entwined behind my back, I floated mindlessly. My eyes were closed, but I felt the roundness of my pregnant stomach protruding out from the surface of the water. The heat of the sun on my skin caused me to smile.

I felt Nathan's familiar mouth as it pressed against my own and opened my eyes, peering up at my husband as he pulled away. "How did I ever get so lucky?" he asked.

"I don't know, how did you?" I asked him playfully, still floating.

He grabbed my waist and spun me around, forcing me into an upright position. "Wanna know a secret?" he inquired.

I shrugged as he wrapped his hands around my waist and pulled me as close as my stomach would allow.

"I sold my soul to be with you," he confessed.

"Seems like a fair exchange." I smiled and leaned in to let our lips touch each other again. This time, I felt Nathan's tongue slip past my teeth, and I allowed myself to sink into his *arms more, now equally being carried by Nathan and the buoyancy of the water.*

"I couldn't agree more," he growled as his mouth moved down to my bare neck, and he slipped a single strap of my bathing suit from my shoulder.

Grabbing my chest, I gasped for air as I struggled to break free from the hold of the dream. I wanted to scream in frustration that my subconscious had allowed the memory of Nathan to surface in my sleep.

Mornings started early in prison. Breakfast was from six fifteen until seven fifteen. My block was usually called around six fifty, and everyone had ten minutes to eat. I'd thought that was impossible when I had first arrived, but I quickly realized you learn to do what you have to when it comes to survival.

I made my bed and headed toward the cafeteria when I heard the announcement for my block's mealtime.

Ruby approached me from behind. "What's with you?"

I shook my head. "What do you mean?"

"You've been quiet since that lady came to see you." I'd told Ruby about Dr. Powell's visit. It had been one week since I'd met her, and I wasn't convinced she'd show up that day, per our agreement. She wanted those papers signed, but I knew better than anyone how hard it was to feel like you were betraying Nathan.

"I've just been thinking about what I'm going to say to her."

Ruby shook her head with a disapproving expression on her face.

"What?" I asked.

"You think this woman's gonna help you?" Ruby asked as we approached the food line. We weren't supposed to talk in the food line, but if you did it quietly and didn't make eye contact, the guards tended to be pretty lenient.

"Maybe," I replied as I started to doubt myself for telling Ruby about my plans.

"Your old man is boning her. I don't see why she'd help you," she stated as she twisted a strand of her red hair around her finger, wearing a puzzled look on her face.

"Boning?" I questioned as I rolled my eyes at the juvenile expression.

"What?" She chuckled. "Would you prefer making love?" she added in a mocking tone as she fluttered her eyelashes.

"I'd prefer not thinking about it at all," I admitted.

"We can call it something else," Ruby continued, quite proud of herself. "They're having a little afternoon delight or bumping uglies, burying the weasel, knocking boots." I'd started to laugh by that point. "No wait, I know. How about bruising the beef curtains?"

"Oh my God," I said as I tried my best to stifle my laughter. "We're getting ready to eat."

She shrugged. "Just trying to be respectful of your feelings."

"Well, don't worry about my feelings when it comes to that bastard. She can have him." I anxiously started to pick at a piece of dried cuticle around my thumbnail, frowning at the look of my unmanicured hands. "And you're wrong. Once Dr. Powell realizes she's engaged to a narcissistic asshole, she'll be all too happy to help me," I explained again.

Ruby shrugged. "You said your man has money?"

"Some, I guess." I attempted to downplay our wealth.

Her voice was high-pitched and innocent now. "Just saying, I doubt I'd care what a man did if he were going to be my meal ticket for the rest of my life."

"I doubt she needs a meal ticket," I bit back as I lifted my tray for my serving of scrambled eggs.

"You know more than me about your type of people, I guess," Ruby whispered as she spied one of the guards watching us. "I'm just saying, I'm not sure I'd be too eager to help out some person I didn't even know if it meant I was gonna lose my man."

"What if you found out that man was a killer?"

She shrugged. "I ain't his judge."

"I just need to make her see that he'll eventually do the same thing he did to me, or worse." When I said the words, an image flashed through my mind of the crime scene photos the detectives had shown me while I was being interrogated. For Evelyn's sake, I hoped Ruby was wrong.

The day's duties seemed to drag, the minutes ticking by at an agonizingly slow pace. Until finally, I heard the beckoning on the speaker that it was time for our area's visiting hours. I wasn't confident Evelyn would be there until I stepped foot into the room and saw her sitting at one of the small round tables.

She smiled at me as I walked toward her and then stood briefly, unsure how to handle our initial greeting. She wore a white blouse and navy-blue blazer with matching slacks that belled out at her ankles. A pair of strappy black heels that looked like they were brand new were on her feet. She didn't dress like me. Well, like I had before. She didn't do her hair like me. She reminded me nothing of myself or, for that matter, of the woman Nathan had taken on as a mistress.

"Elizabeth, hello," she offered in a friendly voice.

"Call me Liz," I corrected her.

"Oh, Liz," she repeated with a hint of excitement.

I laughed in the smug defensive way Nathan had always told me he hated before I added, "I mean, after all, you are sleeping with my husband, so the formality seems a bit silly." Evelyn wasn't the enemy. Nathan was, and I reminded myself to focus on that.

"I'm—" The doctor choked on her words as she watched me take a seat, hovering in midair, unsure how to react to my biting statement.

I forced a smile. "I'm joking. I guess it wasn't very funny."

She paused a little longer before she finally sat. A strained smile found its way onto her face, and she nodded uneasily.

I studied her, then licked my lips, and stated in a flat tone, "If you're not laughing in here, you'll go crazy."

She furrowed her brows as she tucked a strand of hair at the nape of her neck into the bun. "Is everything okay?"

I sighed. "Besides being in prison for a crime I didn't commit? Just peachy. Honestly, I guess I'm just a little surprised you came."

"I told you I would," she replied, straightening her back.

"And Nathan said he would always love me, but then he framed me for murder. I guess I don't trust what people say these days."

Evelyn's head tilted. "I know you have no reason to believe me, but Nathan does care about you."

"What the fuck is wrong with you?" I asked as I shot Evelyn a sharp glare. "You're supposed to be marrying this man, and you're coming here telling me how he cares about me? What's your game, lady?"

She shook her head. "I'm sorry, I don't even know what I'm saying. I'm just so nervous."

"Why are you nervous?"

"Just being here, I feel like I'm lying to Nathan," she started. "All I meant was I can tell he must still care about you."

"Yeah? And you don't think that statement is just a bit messed up from every angle when it's coming from his new fiancée?"

She sighed, and her eyes softened. "I was just trying to make you feel better."

"Well, save it. I don't need you to try to make me feel good about any of this. I'll feel better when I'm no longer serving life for something I didn't do," I replied sharply.

"You're right. I shouldn't have said that." This woman was so nice it was almost infuriating. "I can't imagine what you must be feeling."

The plain truth was I needed her.

I shook my head. "I don't think anyone can understand how it feels to be imprisoned for something you didn't do unless you've been through it. I didn't mean to snap at you. I'm sorry," I offered as I reminded myself why I'd invited Evelyn back to speak to me in the first place. If my plan worked, we could help each other. I would rescue her from being Nathan's next victim, and she could help me find my freedom.

"You don't have to apologize," Evelyn said as she offered me a weak smile. She hadn't directly said if she believed I wasn't the murderer, yet somehow, she made me feel like an ally. I'd considered that perhaps it was just wishful thinking or the skills of her trade shining through and refused to let myself get my hopes up too early.

"Did you know we met at a Halloween party?" I asked, changing the subject.

She shook her head, relaxing in her seat. "Nathan doesn't like to talk about his past."

My mouth turned up into a smile as I silently recalled how handsome he looked that first night when I saw him. No matter how much I hated him now, I had to admit he was one of the handsomest men I'd ever met. I'd told him he wasn't my type. I told him his looks were not typical of the men I dated, but I'd been lying when I said that to him. He was exactly my type—a thick head of chestnut brown hair that begged one to run their fingers through it. The night we'd met, he'd had the perfect amount of facial scruff to appear well kept while at the same time coming off as ruggedly masculine. The younger me was determined to resist him, but Nathan only took that as more of a challenge.

"It was in college," I started. "My friends convinced

me to go to a party at one of the fraternities. I'd sworn off frat boys my sophomore year after one too many had broken my heart, but I suppose time heals all wounds. That or I'd had enough drinks by that point in the evening, and I didn't care anymore."

"I hadn't ever seen Nathan on campus before, which surprised me because he looked like someone who would have caught my attention," I continued. "I suppose since I was an English major and he was seeking a business degree, we didn't exactly travel in the same circles." What I didn't say was that it was more than our majors that divided Nathan and me. Up until college, I had been middle-class poor. Nathan and his mother had been well cared for by Nathan's father, and though he hadn't encountered such a lavish upbringing as many of his friends, he still had a lifestyle far beyond anything I'd experienced.

"At the time I met him, I had no idea, but apparently, I was the other woman. He flirted, and I resisted, but he was so damn charming. Well"—I cocked an eyebrow in her direction—"you know how he is."

She didn't react.

"We spent every moment together for the next two days. Nathan felt like I imagined oxygen would feel after being deprived of it to the brink of death. It was exhilarating, and I'd never felt anything like it." I tilted my head to the side as I recalled the catastrophe that had come next. "It was then that I met his girlfriend at the time. Let's say she wasn't too thrilled to find me in her boyfriend's bed. I was humiliated. Guys like him were the exact reason I hadn't wanted to go to that party in the first place. But it

My Husband's Fiancée

didn't matter. I told him I never wanted to see him again and got the hell out of there. But, like he always does, Nathan worked his magic on me. I was such an idiot."

"We all do stupid things when we're young," she contributed, but I wasn't sure if she was talking about Nathan or me.

"God, when he fixes his eyes on you, it's like you're the only woman in the world. It's fucking intoxicating. It's as if you didn't even know what it meant to be alive before him. When he came crying to me, I should have slammed that door in his face, but instead, I found myself with his arms wrapped around me. Maybe it was young love. It comes on fast and hard, and you don't know how to guard yourself against the pain when you have such limited experience with it." I knew that wasn't it, though. I'd known what I had with Nathan was unique and special. Somewhere along the way, though, we'd become enemies, and he was the kind of man who always won.

"Anyway," I continued as I shook off the memory, "Nathan told me how he never went to that party intending to meet someone, especially someone like me, and he had ended it with his girlfriend the moment I stormed out."

"So you forgave him?"

"Not without making him work for it, but eventually." Against my best intentions, I allowed a moment of tenderness for Nathan to show. "Sometimes, he could be the sweetest man. He told me that he wished more than anything that his mother was still alive when he met me because—"

"He knew his mom would have fallen in love with you

as much as he had?" Evelyn groaned with a defeated look in her eyes.

"Are you kidding me?" I should have known it was a line. Nathan had always been a smooth talker. His mother had passed away his sophomore year in college, and the way he'd always spoken of her, I could tell how much she meant to him. It was easy to feel scattered by the compliment. I sighed. "Don't feel bad. Even I fell for that one."

Evelyn shook her head. "I can't believe that about him."

I shrugged. "Unfortunately, it doesn't matter what you believe. Nathan is happy to destroy your life, even if you don't believe him capable. Look, I understand." I lifted one hand and shook it in the air. "I didn't see it, not even when I found out he was having an affair. I didn't see how dangerous he was until I found myself in here."

Evelyn swallowed hard and hesitated for a moment. "Maybe he said the same thing to both of us. It doesn't mean we won't be happy."

I was the one in prison, yet suddenly, I felt sorry for her. I understood all too well how intoxicating Nathan could be. He was a fantastic lover and had the unique ability of making you feel like you were the most important person in the world. He had a way of making you not want to see what lurked under that passion.

"I'm guessing Alison felt the same way as you." When I spoke the name of Nathan's dead mistress, I felt my stomach lurch forward as though it were an engine stalling. Saying her name always reminded me of the part

I played in her death. While I hadn't killed her, I couldn't help feeling I wasn't entirely innocent either.

Before the doctor could reply to my statement, an announcement on the room speaker warned that visiting time was nearing an end and all inmates should wrap up their conversations. I was still startled to hear myself referred to as an inmate. I wasn't sure it was something I would ever get used to. While the day-to-day routines of my incarceration had become my new normal, I wasn't sure I would ever feel at ease with my new title.

Evelyn stood. She was avoiding eye contact with me. I worried perhaps I'd pushed her too far, comparing her to Nathan's victim. Or maybe she realized he'd shared the same sweet nothings with me, and their relationship wasn't as deep as she thought.

She took a step for the door, and I felt my heart climb up into my throat. "Will you be back?" I blurted out, regretting how eager I sounded.

She glanced at me and then at the exit as she considered my words.

"I understand if this is too hard for you to hear." I offered her an out even though it scared the hell out of me to do it.

She tightened her lips and then looked into my eyes defiantly. "Will you keep your word? If I let you tell me your side of things, you'll sign the divorce papers?"

"Of course." My eyes widened. "I mean, if you still want that when I'm done." She was already on her way out of the room before I finished my sentence.

Over her shoulder, she replied, "Then I'll be back."

She was gone, leaving me with my mundane routine.

Evelyn wasn't just a means to break up the hours of boredom, though. I wanted her help to get out of this place, but as I shared with her the story of how I met Nathan, I realized how much I wished I'd had someone to warn me away from him. The doctor could pretend that our conversation hadn't rattled her, but I could see past her pretending. I would help her see the monster my husband was. Even if I couldn't save myself or Alison, maybe there was a chance I could help her.

∽

3

I stared at the letter in front of me, wondering when Dr. Powell had written it. It had to be soon after we'd spoken. Otherwise, it wouldn't have arrived so quickly. Something I said must have haunted her. It was the only explanation. The excitement began to tingle throughout my body as hope started to build inside me.

I could see her in my mind as she walked briskly to her car, her cheeks flushed and her heart pounding as she replayed our conversation in her head. Did she head straight home so she could put pen to paper? Perhaps she was too concerned Nathan would find out what she was up to that she felt she had to write me here. Was she starting to question the man she'd been so sure she loved? Maybe she stopped at a coffee shop along the way, desperate to justify how he was different with her. But the letter was it. The letter was proof that I might have been able to get through to her. I might have found someone who would help me.

I grinned as I read her words, pleased at the idea of

turning her against Nathan. He'd ruined my life, and even if I never got out of this hell, I would at least take some satisfaction in ruining his.

Dear Liz,

I have rewritten this letter several times. Even writing your name feels like I'm somehow betraying the man I love. Do I call you Mrs. Foster? Elizabeth? It all feels so wrong. I also know if I don't figure out a way for Nathan and me to move forward from his past, we will never have a future together.

I rolled my eyes at her statement of a future together. I hated Nathan, and it was evident by what he had done to me that he hated me as well. Despite our aversion to one another, I'd realized we were linked since my time in this place. Even if he married another woman, he would never be able to give himself over completely. It was why he hadn't left me when he started the affair with Alison and why he hadn't asked me for the divorce yet. As messed up as we were, we'd found ourselves bound to one another. Perhaps we viewed each other as punishment for the sins we'd committed in our lives, but no matter the motive, something between us made it impossible to let the other go entirely.

I want you to know that I heard you. I listened to the truth that is very real for you, but you have to understand I've also gotten to know this man we share. He's kind and loving and generous. I'm confident he could never harm a woman in any way.

He told me he believes the weakness he had in allowing things with Alison to develop is what led to all of this. I'm not naïve. I know he had an affair. If he had not had an affair, you would not have felt you had no other choice but to do what you did.

Do what I did? Maybe I wasn't getting through to her. Perhaps the idea that she would be the one to help me prove Nathan was the killer was a fantasy.

That being said, this is his reality now. This may be the last time we talk. I can't shake the feeling that coming to see you dishonors the man I will marry despite the best of intentions. Even if you can't find forgiveness for what Nathan did, I hope you can at least have the grace to let him move forward with his life. I think it would help you move on as well.

Sincerely,

Evelyn

I squeezed my eyes shut. She was correct in one thing. I hated him. I would never forgive him, but not for what she implied. An affair. I'd decided on the night of the murder I could forgive him for being with Alison. What he did, though, what his dear, sweet Evelyn wasn't willing to see, and what I could not forgive him for was framing me for murder. Unfortunately for Evelyn, it was starting to look like she would go down the same path that had led me to where I was.

What surprised me the most as I'd read Evelyn's words was how sad they made me. Sad to admit that Nathan had won. Sad to think this seemingly sweet woman would be pulled into his darkness. Sad that he would have a life with this woman while I rotted in here for his crimes. My heart ached, and my chest began to tighten as I felt the glimmer of hope I'd allowed myself to feel start to disappear.

4

Mornings were hard. When I'd wake up, I was back home in my bed for a moment with Nathan's warm, strong arms wrapped around me and his breath on my neck. The warm glow from the blinds coaxing me into consciousness.

Then the realization would always hit me when I shifted awkwardly in the bunk that was just slightly too small for me to be comfortable. I would shiver when the cool air hit me, having sometime in the night pushed off the scratchy standard-issued blanket. I'd quickly pull the blanket up under my chin and curl my body tight into a fetal position, despite knowing that any moment the announcements would start the day. Every morning felt the same as I waited for the lingering bond to my past life fade from my subconscious.

In the beginning, I'd spent my time wondering what Nathan was doing. As realization of what he had done to me and to Alison set in, those curiosities were gone. But something changed when Evelyn came to see me. I started wondering about him again. Were they living together? Was he holding her in the morning now instead of me? I was so fucking angry with myself that I let the curiosities find their way into my brain.

Evelyn was not his type. Alison, at least I understood. She was every man's type, but Evelyn? She was pretty but also looked prickly. Nathan needed a soft hand, a gentle and loving woman who would always reassure him what a fantastic man he was. It was a small price to pay to have him worship you.

Pushing the blanket off, I sat upright, shaking my head, and muttered, "*Goddammit.*" I was determined not to let that man back into my thoughts.

"You okay?" I heard Ruby whisper.

I nodded. "I'm fine." The morning announcements began, and it was time to get up and make our bunks.

"Look, you don't have to tell me if you don't want to, no skin off my nose," Ruby huffed as she proceeded to make her bed in a way I knew I would only have to remake when she wasn't looking to prevent our block from losing privileges.

I huffed. "What?"

"Something's buggin' you, but it's fine if you don't wanna tell me. I was just trying to be nice."

Ruby wasn't wrong. Evelyn coming to see me had stirred up all kinds of feelings about Nathan. "I'm sorry; I know you are. I think I've been kind of upset by this whole situation with Nathan's new fiancée."

Ruby shook her head. "Why you even talk to that woman? Fuck that bitch."

I heard Marla snicker behind me, but I chose to ignore her.

"It's not that simple—"

"Seems pretty damn simple to me," Ruby hissed. "Some ho comes up in here, talking about how she wants me to give up my man without a fight. That'd be the death of her."

"You got that right," Marla bellowed before letting out a belly laugh.

Despite knowing it was probably better for me to keep my mouth shut, I couldn't stop myself. "My husband killed the last woman he had a relationship with. If I don't try to talk some sense into her, there's a good chance he could do the same with her," I argued.

"Then she got what she deserved for messing around with a man who wasn't hers," Ruby spouted, not hiding her annoyance with Dr. Powell.

"He's not my man anymore!" I snapped.

"You still married?" Ruby asked.

"Well yes, but—"

"Then he's your man," Ruby replied matter-of-factly.

"I don't think that's quite fair," I said, a little surprised I was so eager to defend Evelyn.

"Nah." Ruby clicked her tongue in disapproval. "That's something a woman don't do to another woman."

"Oh, but killing a woman is okay?"

"I didn't say that," Ruby defended herself. "Just you shouldn't be surprised if you're shady behavior leads to you gettin' got."

"Getting got?" I repeated in disbelief. The words sounded foreign coming out of my mouth. "A woman doesn't deserve to die because she had an affair with someone."

"Yeah, Ms. Bougie," Marla chimed. "What makes you this lady's savior anyway? She seems to know exactly what she's getting herself into, and she's just fine with it."

I wanted to snap at Marla and tell her to shut the hell up because I didn't ask her opinion, but I would never say that, especially to her. Instead, I conceded. "Maybe you guys are right."

But they weren't right. I needed to figure out some way to help save Evelyn's life. Maybe if I could figure out a way to do that, I wouldn't feel so guilty about the role I played in Alison's death.

Library duty was the best part of my day. The more senior inmates always chose to take the job of re-shelving or whatever the librarian had for them that didn't require too much effort. Cart duty was considered the worst, but I loved it. I got to curate the picks, and then I went around to pass out books to inmates. I would get to tell them about what story I thought they'd like the most. I think it was what made a lot of the women in here like me. It was a way to get to know and connect using something I enjoyed.

One girl I'd recently met had been a particularly hard puzzle for me to solve. Savannah was very young and terribly quiet. At first, I'd thought she was scared, but I had quickly realized it was sadness dripping from her. She usually took a hard pass on books from me, but I thought I might have finally figured out what would resonate with her after chatting with other ladies and piecing together a bit of Savannah's story.

"Hi." I smiled at Savannah as I approached with my cart, pulling to the left to account for the one wobbly wheel.

Savannah didn't like to leave her bunk if it wasn't required. She never really wanted to talk to anyone, but something about her reminded me of myself in a way. After weeks of small conversations with her, I had extracted that she came from a smaller town. When she was a senior, she and her boyfriend found themselves pregnant. Shortly after graduation, she had the baby. It was hard on them, but they were figuring things out.

Now the rest of the story I gathered from bits and pieces I'd heard from other women. The story went that Savannah lost her baby to SIDS. She blamed her boyfriend, saying he never really wanted the baby, and she snapped, burning down his family home. Nobody died, but since the family was sleeping, the prosecutor went after an attempted murder charge. It felt like bullshit to me, but I hadn't had much faith in the legal system based on my own experience.

I got it, though. I understood how Savannah felt. I wanted someone to blame after every miscarriage. Especially after I managed to give birth to a living child, only to lose him hours later, I felt like I wanted the world to burn. Most of the time, I blamed myself, but I think I eventually started resenting Nathan. He would be sad and then somehow find the strength to pick himself up and carry on. I hated how easily he seemed to process his grief while, for me, it felt like a dark hole I only continued to slip further and further into. I knew Savannah's pain probably better than anyone else in this place.

Losing a child was the hardest thing any mother could go through. Nothing was comparable.

"Hey Liz, you seem in a good mood today." Her voice was even, and she barely looked at me when she spoke.

Grabbing a book from my cart, I sat next to the young girl on the bed. "Do I?" I asked, a little surprised that I did find myself suddenly in a decent mood. All day, as I had pushed my cart from block to block, I had been planning out the letter I would write to Evelyn. The letter was going to convince her to keep pursuing the truth about Nathan. Maybe that was what had shifted my mood. "I guess I am. Maybe it's because I've found a book I know you're going to enjoy."

Forcing a tight-lipped grin, she glanced at the pink cover and then back out the window across from her bunk. "Thanks, but I'm still not really in the mood to read anything."

I got that. When I was in the thickest of my depression, I didn't even want to eat. Hell, sometimes walking to the bathroom felt like such a chore I ended up with a UTI infection from holding my urine too long. "Oh," I started, measuring my words carefully. If Savannah was like me, she needed to be handled the same way you would an injured animal. Any sudden movements would send her off, running to hide somewhere. But if I offered her a bite of sustenance and allowed her to choose to take it from me, maybe I could help her find her way out of the darkness she was in. "I completely understand."

"Thanks," she whispered.

I pulled the book close into my body and clutched it

to my chest. "Honestly, I was already on the fence about recommending this one to you."

"Huh?" Her attention was suddenly engaged, and her eyes fixed on mine. "What do you mean? I thought you knew I'd enjoy it."

"Oh, you would, but—well, I mean, if any book should come with trigger warnings, it's this one," I half-joked.

"Trigger warnings?"

I had her. She wanted to know more, so it was just the opening I needed. "Yeah." Tilting my head, I tucked the book under one of my legs and watched her eyes as she followed it. "Don't get me wrong, it's amazing, but it's also a major grab-your-tissues kind of book."

"Really?"

"It's cool." I smiled. "You don't have to humor me. I get sometimes we don't feel like reading." I started to get up but paused when her mouth opened.

"No, really, I'd like to hear what it's about," Savannah insisted.

"You're sure?" I asked, and she nodded. I pulled the book out from its hiding spot and placed it between us. She didn't reach for it, but I watched her studying the cover. "Now, I don't know. Maybe it was such an emotional and hard read for me because of my battles with depression."

"You had depression?"

"Oh, yeah," I replied without hesitation. "After my son died, things got pretty dark."

Savannah was no longer staring at the book. Instead, her eyes were fixed on me. "You lost your son?"

I swallowed hard and felt my eyes grow wet. I had finally processed the grief, but by no means did it make the ache of the loss any less. "I did. He was only a few hours old when he died. I blamed myself and my mother and my husband and anyone who stood still long enough for me to blame them. I even blamed God."

Savannah shrugged and looked back at the book. "That doesn't seem so crazy to me."

"I guess not."

"Why would you want to read a book so triggering for you?" she inquired, the book now finding its place in her hands.

I clicked my tongue as if I was thinking, though I already knew the answer to the question. I knew the moment I'd decided to suggest the book to her. "I think something about seeing someone on a journey to put the pieces of themselves back together again is inspiring."

"*Girl in Pieces.*" She read the title out loud.

"Well, I better get," I said, standing and reaching out my hand to retrieve the book. "Maybe you'll feel up to it next time."

She pulled the book in close. "I mean, if you think I'll like it . . ."

"I don't want to pressure you into reading something if you don't feel up to it. Don't worry, you won't hurt my feelings," I insisted, knowing full well Savannah had already decided she was going to read the book.

She shrugged. "No, it's fine. I guess I can give it a try."

"Okay, if that's what you want." I smiled and returned to my cart. "I better get back to it." As I walked away from Savannah, I noticed that she was already flipping through and skimming pages from the corner of my eyes. Being on cart duty didn't just give me something to fill my time. In some small way, I felt I was helping the other women in here. I'd always viewed books as an escape, and everyone needed a little escape when they found themselves in a place like this.

Maybe I would be able to help Evelyn too and, by extension, perhaps even help myself. I just needed to figure out what I could say in a letter to get her to come back for an in-person visit. If I could inspire Savannah to read the book, I could find the words to reach Evelyn.

∽

5

Dear Evelyn,

After receiving your last letter, I considered not writing back, but ultimately, I felt I had no other choice. Something sent you back here after that first visit, seeking answers from me. I can't believe it was solely because you want my signature on some documents. In my bones, I know you feel it. That something isn't quite right.

Nathan can file for the divorce without my consent, and considering he hasn't visited me inside of these walls a single time, I can guarantee you he is not avoiding this approach out of any loyalty to me. If these are the lies he's feeding you, I think you already know the truth you were seeking. Nathan is manipulating you, but to what end, I am unsure.

Despite how much it makes me uncomfortable to say, I can tell you're nothing like Alison. If anything, you're more like me, and that's what makes us conversing all the more dangerous. We may not look alike, but it is already apparent to me that we might think alike. If he even senses in the least you *suspect him of not being who he says he is, your life could be in danger too.*

Nathan is perfect at reading people. It's a skill he has possessed since I met him. I told him in the first week of our dating I would never get married. My mother is a bitter woman because of my biological father leaving her. I'd decided when I was a kid that marriage wasn't for me. I would never allow someone the opportunity to hurt me. Nathan never pushed the issue.

Grand gestures of love were empty and just a desperate way for unhappy people to prove they were the perfect couple. I never spoke about my feelings, but somehow, he knew. We had only been dating for three months, but it felt like I had known him my entire life. On a day like any other, I arrived to find him waiting for me. He said he missed me and he just wanted to spend time with me. After a full day of classes, I was exhausted and suggested we relax with a movie, comfy clothes, and a big bowl of buttery popcorn.

He was more than happy to oblige my request and even took it upon himself to make the popcorn while I slipped into my sweatpants and an oversized T-shirt. When I came back downstairs, I noticed a book next to him. I went straight for it and asked what it was. The cover read Our Story.

I opened the cover to discover he had created a picture book. He told me it was something he'd been working on and asked what I thought of it. He'd hired someone in the art department to illustrate what was indeed our story. Though it had been a brief relationship, I suddenly realized it was packed with experiences as I flipped through the pages of his creation. The concert we'd gone to where our car broke down in the middle of nowhere and we had to camp out until the following morning. The meals we had cooked together. The time we got locked into the campus library overnight after sneaking off to a supply closet for a quickie.

I smiled and laughed and even shed a couple tears as I flipped through the pages that showed me how much of an adventure our first three months together had been. When I reached the final page, there was a picture of Nathan down on one knee proposing to me. I looked over to find him already kneeling, a ring box perched in his fingers.

He'd said to me, "Liz, I've never felt anything like this in my life. I knew from the start you were different, and every day with you only confirms that instinct. You're my best friend, and there's nobody I'd rather see how this story ends with than you. Will you marry me?" Had he proposed in any other way, I'm not sure I would have said yes.

Yes, it was very romantic, but I can see now that Nathan knew exactly how to propose to get me to say yes. He knows how to get what he wants. He was the one who convinced us to start trying to have a baby in the first place. Everyone who knew us was so surprised to find that detail out. I didn't think I wanted a baby until it was hard for us to get pregnant. He was perfect through it all. Everything changed though, when we lost Matthew.

I hope you'll consider coming for another visit. I think if you don't see this through, you could genuinely find yourself regretting it.

-Liz Foster

I folded the letter, placed it in the envelope, and addressed it to the return address on the letter she had sent to me, which was a PO Box. I put it in the bin of outgoing mail, confident that Evelyn would not be able to resist learning what happened after Nathan and I lost our son.

∽

6

I nibbled on the corner of a piece of burnt dry toast as my mind wandered to what the day would hold. I wasn't sure if the letter I'd written had reached Evelyn yet or, for that matter, if it ever would. If she had received it, would she be willing to listen to what I was trying to tell her? Nathan had a way about him. You wanted to believe him, follow him, and go all-in on anything he asked of you.

"Morning," Ruby chimed as she placed her tray on the table next to mine. She hovered her hand over my apple, waiting for my nod. After, she placed it next to the orange on her tray. Ruby had a sweet tooth, and while chocolate was her favorite, she was happy to accept sugar in all forms.

I stared at my plate and shifted the scrambled eggs around, never taking a bite. Desperately I searched the breakfast food for some clarity, but instead of the answers to the meaning of life, I only saw the bland existence that I was trapped in.

"How's it going?" Ruby asked, digging into her meal with much more enthusiasm than myself.

I shrugged. "Good, just thinking."

"God, don't tell me, 'bout Dr. Bitch again?" She huffed in response and rolled her eyes. I could tell she was growing tired of my worries that Evelyn would not return.

"I know you think she's evil because she's dating my husband, but look at it from her perspective," I argued. "As far as she knows, Nathan's a victim in all this. I'm in here for life, so he's basically single."

"You dead?" Ruby asked, crumbs spraying from her mouth as she did. "'Cause last I checked, you ain't divorced, and you ain't dead. That means he's off-limits, and she's a bitch."

I couldn't stop myself from smiling. I loved that I'd only been friends with Ruby for less than a year, but somehow, she had come to mean so much to me. Time in prison is different than it is in the everyday world, though. Besides the fact we spent so much time together, in a way we had to rely on each other in here. Nobody else was going to look out for you. You needed friendships, or you weren't going to make it.

"What're you grinning at?" she asked.

"You're protective of me," I chimed and nudged her playfully with my shoulder.

"You keep telling yourself whatever you need to," Ruby replied, scooping the last of her eggs onto her toast.

"And yes, I was thinking about the doctor since you asked so nicely. I was just wondering if she would be here today for visitation."

"I don't know why you feel the need to try to save this woman."

"It's not about saving her," I insisted. I lowered my voice and leaned closer to Ruby before I continued. "If I can convince her that Nathan isn't what he says he is, maybe she'll help me find the evidence to show he set me up."

Ruby chewed her bite as she mulled over my words. She turned and looked me in the eyes. "Even if you convinced her, why would she risk her neck to save you?"

My back stiffened. Ruby was right. At first, I was worried she wouldn't want to give Nathan up, but even if she did, why would she risk her safety to save me? If somehow I managed to convince Evelyn that Nathan was a liar, she would leave him. If she thought he was capable of murder, she wouldn't dare cross him. She doesn't know me. Why would she take the risk to help me?

"I have to try." The words crawled out of my mouth, dripping with desperation.

She shrugged.

"Is your sister coming today?" I asked, eager to change the subject.

"Supposed to," she answered as she continued to chew her food. The woman wasn't technically Ruby's sister. They had been placed in the same foster home growing up and had formed a bond. I understood that. My best friend Emily had been closer to me than my sister. I trusted her more than anyone else in my life.

"I bet you're excited," I said.

Ruby smiled, and her eyes widened. "Last time, she

said she was going to see if she could get some of my favorite chocolate bars approved."

I forced a smile, though I already knew that Ruby would be disappointed. There was a strict no food or drink policy when it came to visitors. You could ask for an exception, but they were rare. When they were younger, Ruby's sister was eventually adopted by a family originally from Canada. Whenever Ruby would see her sister on the outside, she always brought her a particular chocolate bar her parents would get shipped in from Canada. The commissary had Hershey bars. That was it. They used to have Snickers, but they were banned when one inmate tried to poison another with a peanut allergy.

"That sounds amazing," I said before I stood and cleared my tray to start my day.

As the day progressed, I watched the hands on the clock tick by, trying to push Ruby's words out of my thoughts. She was right, even though I didn't want to admit it to myself. Even if Evelyn believed me, she still had zero motivation to help me.

I'd once trusted that the evidence would free me, but that hadn't worked out so well. I thought the jury would see that the evidence was circumstantial. To the jury, though, there were too many coincidences. With no new evidence, my original conviction stood little chance of being overturned during an appeal. Accepting that was my fate—to wither in this place until I died—was more than I could carry through. I needed that hope—the hope that Evelyn brought me—even if it was a long shot.

"Liz Foster." I heard my name. "Visitor's room." The guard we referred to as Red stood waiting to escort me.

Her hair was salt and pepper in color, and I assumed she had received her nickname from the fact that her cheeks were always bright red. Or maybe in a life before our paths had crossed her natural hair color had been red. My heart started beating wildly in my chest as Red escorted me down the hall to the visitation room.

The only people who ever visited me besides Evelyn were my lawyer, which wasn't very often, and my mother, but she tended to only come once a month, so it was too soon to be her. When I approached, I peered through the glass. I could see her. Evelyn. She looked different. This time, she was wearing jeans and a form-fitting jersey T-shirt. Her hair was still pulled back, but it was looser in a ponytail instead of a bun.

I entered the room and crossed over to the table. She didn't speak. She only watched as I sat and looked around the room at all the other inmates with their loved ones.

"Did you get my letter?" I asked, breaking the silence between us.

She nodded. "I did." I waited for her to say something else, but she didn't.

I sucked in a breath and prepared to speak when I noticed a slight tremor in Evelyn's hand. She was shaking. It was subtle, but it was there. Was she afraid? Was she scared of me, or had something happened with Nathan? She caught sight of me watching her hand and quickly adjusted, wringing them together to shield the tremor.

"Are you okay?" I asked at last.

She forced a slight smile. "Of course."

I straightened in my seat. Something was different,

and I needed to fish out what it was. "Thanks for coming to see me again," I offered.

She leaned back slightly and crossed her arms. "Honestly, I almost didn't. I want to be very upfront with you," she continued.

I nodded in acknowledgment. "I wouldn't have it any other way."

"I don't see Nathan as you describe him. He has never been anything but kind and loving, and I do plan to marry him. I know you think he's lying about why he's not ready to file for the divorce, but I believe him. I think maybe I have given you the wrong impression somewhere along the way."

"Wrong impression—" I repeated the words. "What do you mean?"

"I'm here because I think if you sign the divorce papers, it will lessen the pain he's going through, and that's what matters to me." Her eyes were fixed on me with a disturbing amount of concentration. I shifted from side to side as if it somehow helped me in dodging her probing glare.

She was doubling down on him. I couldn't blame her. I probably would have done the same if I were in her shoes and didn't know what I did.

At that moment, I felt desperate, but I didn't dare reveal that to her. "I understand. And you're right. Nathan can be very kind and loving. I remember when I had to start fertility treatments, he was amazing. The perfect husband. He made sure I always felt loved and treasured, especially when we would get a negative pregnancy test. He would be sure to take the day off and spend it with me." I didn't like retelling the stories of Nathan that cast him in a positive light. I worried they would muddle her view of him.

"I'm sorry you went through that," Evelyn stated, uncomfortably looking away from me as she tucked a stray strand of hair behind her ear. "It's good you had someone like him to help you."

I paused and focused on steadying my breathing before I continued. *Someone like him to help me.* Her words echoed in my ears. I wasn't helping Evelyn see him for the monster he was. I was painting him as the hero. "Thank you. It was hard on both of us."

"Nathan isn't all bad, and I know that," I continued. "I wouldn't have fallen in love with him if he was. I remember when he texted me an address and asked me to meet him. I pulled up to a beautiful grand white Tudor that looked like it was straight out of a fairy-tale book."

I continued with the story, explaining that Nathan had been sympathetic to how hard infertility had been on me. It wasn't just the hormone roller coaster or the countless negative tests. What continually gutted me were the multiple miscarriages. Knowing that even for a matter of weeks, I carried our child's life inside me only to lose it had me feeling not only grief but also like I was a failure. I'd failed the man I loved. I'd failed our unborn child. I was useless, and I told myself Nathan would eventually see me the way I saw myself.

As I shared the memory with Evelyn, I could see the look in her eyes soften. "I stood in front of that beautiful home, marveling at the well-manicured lawn and wondering who lived there and why Nathan wanted me to meet them. I thought perhaps it was someone from his firm. It was the exact home that one day I had dreamed we would own. It was in one of the most sought-after neighborhoods and had some of the best schools in the state."

As I sat in that seat in prison, I almost thought I could smell the flowers from that day. The entire scene had been perfectly etched into my brain. It had felt like it was from one of the books I'd loved to read. I told Evelyn how I'd been so focused on studying the home I hadn't noticed Nathan walk up behind me. His hand curled around my waist, and he pulled me into him. I moaned slightly.

"You know I could have been a stranger," he whispered against my neck as my body sank against his.

There would never be any mistaking Nathan, though. His presence would fill a room, and the moment I felt his hands on my body, I knew it was him. "Well, if the stranger is as devastatingly handsome as you are, maybe I wouldn't mind."

He gripped me tighter, nibbling playfully at my neck before he said, "Careful, I might think you're serious."

We laughed together as I spun around to greet him. Our lips almost instantly locking against one another. It was hard to believe that even after all the time we had been together, he still gave me butterflies.

"So, who are we here to meet?" I had asked.

"Follow me." He redirected my attention as he gripped my hand and hurried to the front door. He pulled a key from his pocket and slipped it into the lock.

Evelyn sat quiet, enthralled and completely engaged with every single word that left my lips. I told her how

Nathan had purchased my dream home without so much as a hint. I found out later the down payment had come from Nathan's father with the understanding it would be kept a secret.

"He bought you a house to cheer you up?" Evelyn interjected.

"Not exactly," I replied. "I think to Nathan, it was his way of giving me hope. He'd told me he was so confident we would be pregnant by the end of the year, he decided it was time to buy a house for our family. When he said it, I let myself believe him."

"It didn't stop at the house," I continued. "There was a room perfect for the nursery, and if Nathan wasn't at work, he was home, helping me design the perfect space that would... should have one day belonged to our child. Whenever I would say it was silly to be decorating a nursery before I was pregnant, he would tell me that it was essential to finish the nursery now so I could focus on resting when I was pregnant. When. He always used the word. It was never a question to him. At least not at that time."

"I can tell you loved each other," she offered in a soft voice.

"Well, that was a lifetime ago," I said dismissively. "The Nathan that did all those things was either a great liar, or he's changed. Either way, I know what he's capable of now."

She stiffened, shaking her head. "Don't you think there's a chance you might be wrong about him?"

"I'm in here, and he's out there, so no," I answered as I lifted my brows.

She flashed a puzzled expression. "The Nathan you're describing doesn't sound like someone who would do what you say he did."

"It's not what I say he did. He did it," I snapped as my nostrils flared.

"I just don't see it," she insisted, shaking her head. "Everything you've told me paints this picture of a husband who loved his wife."

I huffed, tired of talking in the same circles. If I was going to get Evelyn to see Nathan for who he was, I needed to be vulnerable. To show her that it was at my lowest when he betrayed me. "Did he ever tell you how long it took before we had Matthew?" My lip trembled when I said his name.

She shook her head.

"Our relationship started as a whirlwind. We were engaged after three months, married after eight months, and on our first wedding anniversary, he told me he wanted to start a family. The next seven years felt much longer, though. They were filled with miscarriages and negative tests and trying new doctors until we finally had a pregnancy stick past the first trimester." Nathan wanted everyone who knew him to think of him as the perfect man and, by extension, the perfect husband. It didn't shock me he hadn't gone into details with Evelyn about our fertility battle. It wouldn't have supported the image he preferred to portray. "I think we were both too nervous to be excited when we found out we were expecting."

"I can imagine," Evelyn said sheepishly.

"Nathan was amazing, but things changed, and quicker than I ever thought they could."

"What do you mean changed?"

"I mean, shit got dark and fast after Matthew died." I startled when there was a bell over the loudspeaker, and a voice got on to state visiting time was being cut short due to a disruption in the recreation yard and everyone needed to exit the room in an orderly fashion.

Evelyn's head jerked around the room. She seemed almost panicked that our time was over. "What happened when Matthew died?" she asked, leaning forward.

I stood and shrugged, thinking perhaps if I held on to information Evelyn wanted, she would return. "Sorry, I gotta head out. If you don't listen, they take away privileges."

I started toward the door before I stopped and turned to face Evelyn. She hadn't moved. She was sitting completely still. "I'll see you tomorrow?" I called out.

She exhaled a large breath before she nodded.

∼

7

As I was finishing my meal the following morning, I looked up to see Savannah crossing the cafeteria, headed straight for me. I watched her as she approached, a little surprised by the visit as she didn't typically venture out of her cell. She sat down, and I looked around the room to see if anyone was watching. Savannah didn't talk to people. She preferred to keep to herself.

The young girl stared at me, but she didn't say a word. Her facial expression wasn't much help either.

"Good morning," I said, hoping my words would prompt her to reveal the purpose behind her visit.

"I'm sorry to hear about your baby." Her words caught me off guard. It had been a couple years since I lost him, yet somehow just the mere utterance of the term "your baby" could instantly stir all those painful memories.

I nodded, unable to provide an audible answer right away. We both sat there silently, processing and replaying our pain for a moment.

"I wanted to die when I lost mine," she admitted, in an almost whisper.

I considered reaching out across the table and extending a hand to hold hers, but I decided it wasn't what she was looking for since she was hiding them under the surface of that cold cafeteria Formica. She was searching for the same thing I had once been. Someone to listen to her who wouldn't try to convince her that everything would be okay. Someone who could give her hope she wasn't crazy for feeling the things she did.

"I did too," I admitted.

Her head jerked up, and she peered at me with her large almond-shaped eyes. "Did you ever try it?"

I shrugged. "I don't know."

"You don't know if you ever tried to kill yourself?"

"I know I took enough pills one night that I should have died, but I don't remember making the conscious choice to end things. I just knew I wanted to be able to sleep and not wake up thinking about—about everything I'd lost," I explained.

"Did they try to lock you away after that?" she asked, and I could hear how angry she was at everyone in her life.

I shook my head. "No, my husband found me and got me the help I needed."

"Therapy doesn't work," she huffed.

"It's not a magic bullet, that's for sure, but it's a start, I guess. At least that's what I told myself to keep me going." What I didn't tell her was how I had quit going not long after I started, though I hadn't shared that information with Nathan either. In fact, it had been one of the many mistruths between us.

"And then you were able to just go back to living as if nothing happened?" Savannah's voice hitched, and I could tell she was losing trust in me.

"Oh, hell no. My life is so fucked up because of what happened."

"What do you mean?"

I couldn't believe it as the words left my mouth. I'd talked about Nathan with some of the women before, but never this shit. This was personal, too personal. It made me vulnerable to let people know about this stuff.

"Just between us?" I asked, leaning forward. Her eyes widened as she nodded. "Therapy helped me a little at first, and then I started reading books like the one I gave you. Eventually, I could get up and shower, eat, and function on a basic human level, but it didn't restore my life. My marriage fell apart. I pushed my husband away to the point that he cheated on me. I pushed my mom and sister away. My best friend lived in another state, and I lied to her and told her everything was fine when it wasn't."

"So why keep trying?" Savannah asked.

"Because one of the things I learned from all those books, and yes, even the therapist, was that healing takes time. If I could start taking care of myself again, maybe eventually, I would get through it. One day, I might be able to see some random kid at the park without breaking down into tears. And who knows, maybe one day far enough into the future, I might even have another shot at a family."

"Do you believe that?" Savannah laughed a little. To

her, I probably did look crazy. Eventually, she would get out of this place, and she would still be young enough to have a new life. I didn't plan to grow old here. I would find a way out, but there was no telling what my future might hold when I did.

I sighed. "Sometimes, the only thing that keeps us sane is hoping for what seems impossible."

She pressed her lips together, and I could tell she wanted to tell me something, but she was holding herself back.

"What is it?"

"I didn't try to murder my boyfriend or his family," she whispered.

"What?"

"I went there that night looking for a box of baby stuff I knew his mom had put out in the garage. She just boxed it all up like she was trying to forget she ever had a grandbaby. I was going to take it home with me because she didn't deserve to have those things. When I found the box, I started going through it, and . . . I don't know . . . I guess I just wanted the pain to stop. I got this crazy idea that if I burned all the baby stuff, maybe I could let go as she had."

"Savannah, did you tell this to your lawyer?" I pressed.

She itched her head and nervously looked around. "If I were a better mama, maybe my baby would still—"

"Stop it!" I snapped. "That road only leads to places that will make you crazy."

"By the time I realized the gas can was near the box, it was too late to do anything about it. I should have run in and got them all out, but all I kept thinking was if I just sat there and let the fire take me, it would all be over. The next thing I knew, I was waking up in a hospital bed I'd been handcuffed to," Savannah added.

"It was an accident. You have to tell your lawyer," I insisted.

"It won't do any good," she argued. "I didn't say anything until now, so it'll just look like I'd say anything to get out of this place."

"Do you mind if I reach out to my lawyer about your case?" I asked.

She shrugged. "That's nice of you, but my family doesn't have any money for an expensive lawyer."

"Maybe they can refer you to someone. Is it okay if I at least reach out?"

She huffed as she stared at a scratch on the tabletop in front of her. "I guess. Hope for the impossible, right?"

I smiled. "Exactly."

Savannah had that look again, the pursed lips that said her lips wanted to say something that her brain was telling her she probably shouldn't. I cringed when she finally unleashed the question. "Are you still married?"

It was then that I realized she didn't know my story.

"Technically," I answered at last.

"How can someone be technically married? Do you have a husband or not?"

Marla happened to be walking by at that precise moment and heard Savannah's question. She let out a cackling laugh before she plopped down onto the bench next to me, sprawling her upper body across the table and writhing around as she continued her display.

We both sat and watched Marla until she finally tired herself out. "It means we will be getting divorced," I answered at last.

"Divorced?" Marla squealed as if the word were an absurd option. "I ain't seen him up in here asking for no divorce."

I wanted to climb under the table and hide. Marla was so loud. I felt everyone's eyes in the room fixed on me. As I swallowed, it felt like a group of small pebbles sliding slowly down my throat.

"His new fiancée asking me for it is a pretty good indicator that Nathan no longer wants to be married," I replied, doing my best to sustain my composure.

"Do you still want to be married to him?" Savannah asked.

I hadn't had anyone directly ask me that question before. I wanted to kill Nathan for what he did to me, but somewhere in my insane mind, a tiny part of me missed him while the rest of me wanted to squeeze the last bit of life out of him.

"Of course not," I answered, coming to my senses.

"Oh, you ain't heard about what Liz's man did to her?" Marla asked, to which Savannah shook her head wildly, hanging on to every word Marla spoke. "According to Miss Thing here, he cheated on her, offed his side piece, and then pinned the whole damn thing on her. He got rid of his mistress and his wife in one fell swoop. Now he's got himself a new piece of ass doing his dirty work for him."

"You don't know what the hell you're talking about," I snapped. She wasn't entirely wrong, but Jesus, I wanted to punch Marla in the throat. I knew she was the last person I wanted to have as an enemy in this place, though.

"Is that right?" She chuckled as she stared at me with her mouth hanging open. "Then can you please explain to me who the hell this bitch is who keeps coming in here to get you to hand over your technical husband?"

"What's she talking about?" Savannah asked faintly, obviously intimidated by Marla's presence.

I could tell Marla enjoyed the unease she caused in everyone around her. It was apparent it made her feel powerful. I decided I wouldn't give her the satisfaction. I cleared my throat and pushed Marla's beefy arm out of my way. She seemed shocked I'd touched her, and rather than bring too much attention to the action I had immediately regretted, I answered Savannah's question that had been hanging heavy in the air.

"My husband has gone and gotten himself engaged to a new woman, but he is too afraid to ask me for a divorce. She decided to take it upon herself to obtain one for him," I explained, tossing a quick glare in Marla's direction before I looked back at Savannah, who seemed more confused than ever.

"Why would your husband be too scared to ask you himself?"

"That's an excellent question, Savannah." I forced a smile to go along with my response. "And if I had to take a guess, I would say he doesn't want to face what he's done to me."

"Tell her," Marla taunted. "Tell her what you say lover

boy did to you. Tell her what you say that sick fuck did to his baby."

I looked at Savannah as I tried to determine if she would believe me if I told her the truth. I'd finally decided it was better if she heard it from me than someone else. I didn't want to risk the chance of her thinking this was something I could do.

"Baby?" Her eyes widened when the word squeaked out.

I swallowed. This was going to go one of two ways. Savannah would believe me, or she would suddenly view me as a monster like the rest of the world. I cleared my throat. "My husband got his mistress pregnant. I guess he decided the easiest way out was to kill her and pin it on me."

"I don't understand. Why would he do that? He—" Savannah swallowed the rest of her words.

"I've thought a lot about that exact question. My husband comes from a world that's different than most. I think he thought he would lose everything if it got out that he got a woman who worked for him pregnant. He must have figured out I knew about the affair and decided the safest bet was for him to take us all out."

"But his own child?" Savannah gasped.

Marla hopped to her feet and slammed her hands onto the table, garnering the attention of one of the guards. "The world is a fucked-up place, kid, and if you aren't willing to be the one doing the hunting, don't be surprised if you get hunted." And with those bright and cheery words, Marla moved on to the next group of inmates who had captured her attention.

"Don't listen to her," I said as I shook my head. "Not everyone is like that. Honestly, I didn't think Nathan could ever do something so terrible."

"Are you sure he did it?" Savannah asked.

"I don't know who else could have set me up if it wasn't him," I replied. I had considered it wasn't Nathan who had destroyed my life, but every time I ran through the scenario, there was no other option. At one point, I even thought that maybe Nathan's father was behind everything. He had never approved of me. But then why give the down payment for our house? And what were the odds Nathan would have confided in a man he barely spoke to about an affair he was having? The only person who could have known about Alison and figured out what I had been up to was Nathan. He was also the only one I could see with motive and opportunity. It had to be him. "I wish it weren't."

"What are you going to do?" The quiet Savannah who kept to herself was gone. All she wanted to know was how in the hell I was going to get myself out of this mess. I wish I'd known the answer myself.

"Don't laugh," I warned her. "But I'm hoping I can convince Nathan's new fiancée to look for any evidence that might show Nathan was the one behind all of this."

"Don't you hate her for even coming here and asking you for a divorce?" Savannah asked.

I shook my head. "It's not her fault she fell in love with him. He's the easiest man in the world to fall in love with. Honestly, I feel sorry for her. I can see things she can't yet. She's naïve, just like I was."

"Okay, so you know I hate therapists and all," Savannah started.

"Yes, you've made your opinion clear," I replied, making a mental note never to share with her that Evelyn was a therapist.

"Well, one time, my mama went with me to a session, and that doctor was going on and on to her about how it wasn't my mama's job to save me."

"Well, first off, that's a terrible thing for a therapist to say in front of you," I replied.

"No, it wasn't. I get it. She was right. If I was ever going to be okay, it had to be on my terms, not because my mama wanted it."

"Well, this isn't the same situation. I wouldn't just be saving this woman. I'd be saving myself," I pointed out with a defensive tone.

"As long as you're not trying to take responsibility for other people's life choices," Savannah said. I was impressed by the glimpse of wisdom that came from her. But I couldn't tell Savannah or anyone else for that matter because I did bear responsibility for what landed me in this place. I might not have killed Alison, but I can't help wonder how things would have gone if I had just left Nathan instead of what I did. Would she still be alive? Evelyn was my chance to do it right this time.

"What if I can save this new woman? Shouldn't I at least try?"

"One thing my mama never could wrap her head around was that she couldn't save me because I didn't want to be saved. I'm still not sure I don't deserve to be in here."

"Savannah, don't say that."

"My point is, maybe this woman coming to see you, she doesn't want to be saved. Maybe she's just fine where she's at."

Was Savannah right? Perhaps trying to convince Evelyn that Nathan was a monster wouldn't matter because she didn't care. I refused to allow myself to believe it.

"I have to try," I said.

Savannah stood. "I understand. Just don't be surprised if she prefers to stay in the burning house." She started to walk away before she looked over her shoulder and added, "Oh, and if you have any more books you think I'd like, send them my way."

"Of course," I answered. Savannah could say what she wanted, but deep down, everyone wanted to be saved. Even if they didn't know it.

∽

8

Evelyn made more sense as Nathan's wife than I did, at least on the surface. She was a doctor, and I was the stepdaughter of a fisherman who dreamed of being a writer. That being said, I never had trouble filling the role of Mrs. Foster. I was comfortable playing the hostess, even if I didn't always like it. I understood that our home spoke of Nathan's success, and the appearance of success was required for him in building trust with clients. Despite my never wanting to play the supporting role of the spouse in my youth, I was damn good at it in almost every way.

I did have trouble fulfilling one aspect of my duties as Nathan's wife, though. The absence of breastfeedings and walks in the evening with my perfect husband with our stroller in tow. There were no bedtime stories and no pitter-pattering of little feet as they hurried to the door to welcome daddy home. A part of being the perfect wife to the ideal man was giving him children. I'd decided Nathan eliminated me because I knew too much, but in the back of my mind, I'd wondered if his real reason was because I was defective.

As I entered the room, I saw Evelyn sitting at one of the round tables. She smiled at me, and I wondered how she viewed me. Was I someone who, under different circumstances, she envisioned shopping with on weekends? In another life, was I someone she would have shared stories of the romantic things her fiancé had done for her?

I wasn't her friend, though. I reminded myself of that fact as I crossed the room to take a seat. I was the woman who was standing in the way of what Evelyn viewed as her happily ever after. I admired her for her dedication. She knew what she wanted, and she was willing to do the hard work to get it.

I paused before taking a seat. A young family sitting at the table to the left of Evelyn caught my attention. A gentleman sat next to a little girl in braided pigtails. The woman I can only assume was her mother sat across from her, trying her best to fight back the tears threatening to unleash themselves at any moment. I wondered if he had braided the girl's hair himself. Would Nathan have been the type of father to have learned those things?

"Liz." Evelyn spoke my name as if I hadn't seen her.

I forced a half-smile as I sat down across from her. I noticed something that had been absent before. A new diamond glinted from her finger, and I was sure if it had been there before, I would have noticed. A memory flashed through my mind of Nathan's proposal to me, and I flinched slightly.

"It's beautiful," I said as I nodded toward the oversized piece of jewelry.

She slipped her other hand over the ring before she pulled her hands into her lap. "I'm so sorry," she muttered. "I try to remember to take it off before I come here."

I laughed. "Afraid someone might try to steal it?"

She cleared her throat. "No, I was trying to be respectful of you."

"If it bothered me that you were engaged to Nathan, I would have never asked you to come back." The words fall instinctively off my lips.

She released the ringed finger from its hiding place, and I avoided looking directly at it. I didn't care about the trinket he had given her. I cared about getting out of here.

"So . . ." She cut through the awkward quiet. "I won't lie. The anticipation has been killing me since our last visit."

"Huh?" I feigned confusion.

"Are you kidding?" She gasped. "I was barely able to sleep last night." She hesitated. "You know, about the —baby."

A lump formed in my throat when she hesitated before saying "the baby." It felt like she had reached inside my chest and removed my heart out of my mouth. Sometimes, I was still surprised by how grief could overwhelm me.

I crossed my arms over my chest as if it was somehow a barrier between us, protecting me from her prying. I was a little surprised I didn't want to retell this part of our lives. It was one of the things that impulsively I tried to keep for myself, but I knew if I wanted Evelyn to see Nathan for who he truly was, I needed to bare this part of my soul.

"I'm pretty sure that's when I lost him," I started.

"Nathan?"

I nodded. "You have to understand how much I . . . how much we wanted a baby. We'd lost so many pregnancies before that one. I think both of us were scared to even breathe for the first trimester. I remember on the fourteenth week he brought me home a present. He'd had a silver baby rattle engraved with the name Foster on it. He told me how he bought it before the first miscarriage and that he'd held on to it all this time because he knew one day we would have a Baby Foster."

I moved my eyes down to the table, staring at the various scratches across the top before fixating on a chip along the edge. I couldn't look at Evelyn while I retold the story of when I believe my marriage first fractured.

"We both let ourselves believe that time was going to be different, though, in the back of my mind, I kept waiting for the terrible to happen. At least until I hit twenty weeks. That's when I finally decided we were going to make it. We were going to have the family we'd always dreamed of. None of our previous pregnancies had made it that far."

"I'm so sorry," Evelyn squeaked out.

"It's funny, just before that pregnancy, we had actually started to discuss adoption. Sometimes I wonder if we had gone that route if things would have worked out differently."

"How do you mean?"

"With that last pregnancy, we actually had a child. It wasn't this abstract idea of a baby. We actually held our child in our arms. I started having contractions at twenty-three weeks," I said. "I tried to make an excuse for the first contraction. It was just cramps and completely normal. But the second one had me dialing Nathan instantly. He rushed home from work and took me straight to the hospital. They managed to stop the contractions and put me on bed rest. He didn't leave my side."

"He can be kind of sweet like that." Her words caused me to wince. The familiarity she spoke about him caught me off guard.

I pushed my feelings aside and continued. "I was just so angry. It wasn't fair. The second we were in the hospital, I felt that hope I'd let myself have start to disappear. It wasn't even a week before the contractions started again, and we were back at the hospital. They tried to stop it, to give the baby more time, but it was too late. I gave birth to our son the next day."

"He was alive?"

I nodded. "We named him Matthew after Nathan's uncle. Nathan kept telling me he was going to make it, but he only lived a few hours. That's the only time I've seen my husband weep."

"It must have been so hard."

"I could see it in his eyes afterward. The way he looked at me had changed."

"What do you mean?"

"It was obvious he blamed me," I said as the haunting

way my husband had looked at me that day replayed in my mind.

"Did he ever actually say that?" Evelyn asked.

"Of course not." I scoffed. "Nathan is much subtler in the way he lets people know they've disappointed him. At first, he started to work late a couple nights a week until, eventually, it was almost every night. Honestly, I didn't mind. If he got home late enough, I could already be in bed, so he would never know I hadn't even gotten out of my pajamas during the day."

I looked around at the other inmates. Some were meeting with loved ones, some perhaps family friends. I knew none were meeting with the fiancée of their husband. I laughed as the realization of what was happening settled over me.

"What is it?" Evelyn inquired.

I shook my head. I'd had enough talking about Nathan and Matthew for one day. "Nothing. We should probably wrap things up," I said as I looked at the clock.

"We have twenty more minutes," she stated.

"Actually, I have another visitor today who is waiting to see me," I explained. I didn't. We were only allowed one visitor per day, but Evelyn didn't need to know that.

She looked surprised by the fact someone would be visiting me and perhaps slightly alarmed. Did she think it was her beloved Nathan?

"My mother," I replied through gritted teeth. My mother was actually on the schedule for tomorrow, but the white lie would give me the break I needed.

"Oh, my. I am so sorry. Have I been taking up time that was meant for her?"

I laughed. "Oh no, you're doing me a favor, trust me."

"That bad, huh?"

"Let's just say she's a real piece of work," I replied. And she was. I knew even as a teen that she was a narcissist. She also never hid the fact that she blamed me for my father leaving, though she never bothered to explain her reasoning. She also hated the fact that my stepfather and I had gotten along so well. There was very little about me that my mother did like. Since going to prison, she had tried to be what she called a better mother to me, though I didn't see much of a difference. Unfortunately, I needed her financial help with my appeal. Even my commissary money came from her.

"If it makes you feel any better, most of the people I work with have some level of dysfunction with their family, especially their moms," Evelyn offered.

I tilted my head and studied the woman as she stood to leave. Her form-fitting dress was flattering, but she didn't look like she was comfortable in it, as if it were a new look she was trying out. Despite the discomfort, she did wear it well. I could envision her talking to people about their problems. She was a good listener. I wasn't looking for her to be my shrink, though. "Why would that make me feel better?"

"I'm sorry, I didn't mean anything by it." She seemed alarmed by my response. "I was just trying to say it's normal."

"Nothing about my family is normal," I added.

"So tomorrow?"

"Uhh—" My lie about my mother had already

trapped me. "I have a meeting with my lawyer tomorrow." I quickly stumbled into another lie. "Next week?"

She nodded. "Of course."

∼

9

Dear Evelyn,

I'm sorry I had to cut our last visit short. I, of course, told my mother nothing of you. Can you imagine what the people in our lives would say if they found out we were conversing with one another? Especially Nathan.

I made the statement to Evelyn with clear intentions. I needed her to understand the danger around what we were doing by seeing one another. Nathan had been willing to kill and frame me to protect himself. I was confident he wouldn't hesitate to do it again.

It was challenging to share the story of losing Matthew, but it somehow also felt freeing, if that makes any sense. Last year was consumed by the trial and since then, learning how to survive in this place. When I think about my son now, it's in brief passing before I push his memory aside and try to focus on something right in front of me. After we spoke, though, I haven't been able to get him out of my thoughts. The pain is still there, but I was able to think of the way he looked in my arms that day without crumpling into a heap of tears. Maybe this is what healing looks like. I don't know.

I remember when Nathan sat on the bed next to me as I held our son, and for a moment, we were a family. The pain of that time was so great that I often forget how life was perfect for a few hours.

It didn't stay that way, of course. As we buried our son, I think I also buried our marriage. We would fight over the simplest of things. At first, Nathan would let me yell and stay silent, but he eventually just started to leave when I would have my outbursts. That was when the late nights started, and before I knew what had happened, he was barely around at all.

Our conversation got me thinking about that time and when it all started to slip away from me. The first time I noticed something was when Nathan's company had a party to celebrate the completion of their new office space. It had been about eight months since we lost Matthew. After months of barely seeing Nathan, I decided on a whim that I would surprise him. I'd stopped attending company functions but decided I would get all dolled up and try my best to play the role of his wife again. By his reaction, he was surprised to see me rejoin the living. He told me he assumed I wouldn't be feeling up to it, and he would understand if I wanted to stay home. I thought he was afraid I'd make a scene in front of everyone and break down crying. I practically begged him to take me with him, and I told him that if I didn't get out of the house, I would go crazy.

I didn't realize that wasn't the source of his apprehension at all until we were there. We didn't speak at all in the car, which would have been strange at any other time, but unfortunately, it had become our new normal since Matthew.

He'd been on the committee that made all of the selections with the new building, and I could tell he was proud of how the project had turned out. The building was beautiful. It was a tower of glass and metal that looked like a sculptural work of art. It seemed like a waste to be used for something as dull as a brokerage firm, but it was spectacular, nonetheless.

That wasn't the only beautiful work of art I noticed that night. I saw her immediately. The young blonde on the other side of the room was staring at Nathan with so much intensity I thought she might bore a hole clear through his head. She looked . . . disappointed. He was careful to never look in her direction. I know because I watched all night, waiting for him to sneak a glance. I could tell he was avoiding her.

I'd never been the jealous type because Nathan had never given me a reason before, but looking at her, something within told me I needed to be on alert. I tried to convince myself it was all in my head. Before we left the party, I decided to see how he reacted to me noticing the girl. I took him aside and asked who she was. He pretended he had no clue who I was talking about, and my stomach instantly sank like a stone to the bottom of a lake.

It would have been impossible not to notice her. I wasn't blind. Every person at that party had discovered her plunging neckline and bright red lips. She commanded everyone's attention.

I let my suspicions be known. I clarified and told him I was talking about the blonde who couldn't keep her eyes off him the entire night. His reaction spoke louder to me than his actual words. He'd tossed his hands up and stormed out of the room as he told me how ridiculous I was being. Nathan was always excellent under pressure. I'd never seen him react in such a way. On the drive home, he asked how much I'd had to drink that night and how disappointed he was that we had to leave before I embarrassed us both.

I hadn't been irate. I hadn't made a scene or lost my temper. Nathan was worried, and he was never worried. I knew then something was going on.

I didn't bring it up again. I didn't want to fight—the months since Matthew's death had been hard enough on us. We had been lost so deep in the abyss of our misery we hadn't even celebrated our tenth wedding anniversary. I suppose I didn't want there to be any truth to my suspicions. I pretended at first that she didn't exist, and Nathan and I were okay. Eventually, I couldn't avoid thinking about her, and I had to know. It's funny how much easier pretending is sometimes. If I had just continued to do so, maybe everything would have turned out differently.

Sincerely,
Liz Foster

~

10

One of the things I hated the most about being in prison was not having a way to escape my thoughts. Before, when I would think of Nathan and Alison being together, all I had to do was drink until they were a distant memory. Here, though, behind the miles of fencing, barbed wire, and bars, nothing existed at night but you and your thoughts. It was the truest form of punishment for a person I could have ever imagined.

Pretending was easier on the outside of this place. In here, all those vices that kept the insecurities at bay were stripped away, and you were left with the rawest view of who you were and the life you had lived.

I dropped a hand outside of my cot and let it fall to the cool concrete beneath me, grounding me to the place I was. A reminder I was no longer in that life I'd left behind. In prison, though, all I could do was let the quiet in, which made my thoughts run wild.

"I miss you," I'd said to him the morning after we had

fought at his office reveal party. I wanted to tell him I knew something was going on with the blonde at his office. I wanted to scream at the top of my lungs that I knew he was up to no good, but when I opened my mouth, the only thing that came out were those words. I. Miss. You.

He'd sat down next to me on the bed, and without looking at me, he said, "I miss you too, Liz." His voice had been gentle, and at moments like that, I convinced myself I was crazy and had imagined all of it.

I'd reached out to touch his arm, and he'd pulled away. I stared up at him, my eyes full of pain. "I'm sorry, we'll get there," he'd said to me. I didn't say anything, but with that statement, my suspicions were confirmed. After he'd left for work that day, I went to our bathroom and started looking through everything. I rifled through the hamper, examined the dirty laundry, turned out all the trash bins, and sorted through all the receipts I could find. I didn't know what I was searching for, just that I would know it when I saw it. I searched all day and found nothing. Nothing I could use to prove to I wasn't crazy and knew exactly what he was up to with the blonde.

I flipped to my other side and tucked my arms under the blanket as I squeezed my eyes closed and tried to push the memories from my mind. *Dammit, go to sleep already,* I yelled silently to myself.

~

11

Before library duty, I'd placed my monthly postcards into the outgoing mail drop box. In all honesty, there wasn't much to update people on, so I preferred to send postcards. One would go to my sister, who, before prison, I would never have sent one to, but it seemed to save me from her visiting. She was probably one of the few people in my life I could go without seeing again. To her, everything was always a competition. It was exhausting to listen to her constantly try to measure our lives against each other.

One went to my grandmother, who was probably one of the few people in the world who believed in my innocence. And one went to my best friend since college, Emily. Emily's job had moved her out of state, and since then, the only time we would see one another was on our yearly girls' trips. I missed them.

Emily was a single mom and had a life to protect, but she never made me feel like I was a liability. It probably wouldn't help her skyrocket to the top of the PTA's most beloved mother list if it got out that her best friend was imprisoned for the brutal murder of a pregnant woman.

On this day, though, I'd had one more postcard than usual. I'd also sent one to my mother. She had been there only a few days ago, but the more I thought about it, the more I decided that maybe she could be of some help.

A postcard did not leave a lot of room for me to explain to her the situation I'd found myself in. I knew it would have been better to put it all in a letter, but things tended to work better with my mother when I shared less information with her. She wouldn't like it if she found out I was speaking to Nathan's fiancée. She would go even crazier if she knew my master plan was to turn Dr. Powell into a double agent of sorts.

All of those things aside, my gut told me I was flying blind. I needed to know more about Evelyn and her life if I was going to figure out a way to convince her she was on the wrong side of right when it came to Nathan. I just needed my mom not to realize exactly what she was doing.

Mom,

Thanks for the visit last week, it was very nice to see you. Before you come back, I have a huge favor to ask. There is a woman I think may be able to help my case, but I don't want to reach out until I know more about her. I was hoping you could see what you could find out about Dr. Evelyn Powell. Please be discreet in this matter.

Thank you. Love and miss you,

Lizzy.

I waited for mail delivery, hoping for something from Evelyn, but nothing came. The next day, there was still nothing. The following visitors' day, there had also been no one to see me. A part of me started to worry. Evelyn said she would be back, but what if Nathan had found out Evelyn was coming to see me? How would he have reacted? What would he do if he found my letters?

∽

12

"Are you out of your mind?" I hadn't even made it into the visitors' room when I heard my mother's voice.

I picked up my pace as I crossed the room, careful not to run as the guards disliked that even more than people shouting in their visitors' room.

"Mom," I hissed as I sat down across from the woman who looked much older than her years. "You can't yell in here."

"Oh, I haven't even started yelling," she snapped as she slammed a hand down on a postcard sitting in front of her. She had flipped it, so the words written on it were hidden, but I recognized the cheesy picture on the front of a rainbow over a babbling brook.

I hesitated for a moment. "Why are you so angry?"

"You can't be serious? You're talking to Nathan's new fiancée, and you ask me why I am so angry," she barked.

"How did you find out she was engaged to Nathan?"

"Lizzy, what were you thinking?" she asked as she ignored my question.

"I don't see why you're upset with me. She was the one who came here in the first place," I stated in defense.

"And why on earth would she come to see you?" Mom snapped, but I didn't reply. "How do you think Nathan is going to react if he finds out you've been talking to her?"

"I don't give a shit what Nathan thinks." But that wasn't exactly true. I had been worried about Evelyn's safety.

"Lizzy!" I felt like I was thirteen years old again, being scolded for sneaking cigarettes with the neighbor boy behind the garage. Not that my mother ever had the right to condemn any of my behavior. Dad walking out on us was shitty, but it didn't justify the countless men she'd paraded through our lives on her desperate hunt for someone to take care of us financially. Life with my mother was tolerable after she'd found and married Phil. Unfortunately, my stepdad had died from a heart attack my freshman year in college. Mom's crazy was off the charts after that.

During the trial, she'd met and married her third husband, some small-town Southern Baptist preacher, because, of course, my mother can't bear to be alone in life. They'd met at a prayer group. I could imagine how she told everyone she had been the best mother possible. I knew the truth, though. My mother was still the same manipulative woman who had taught me to use everyone until they were of no further use to you.

"I'm sorry," I whispered as I lowered my gaze. "She

claimed Nathan wanted to file for a divorce, but he's been too concerned to actually do it."

"Concerned?"

"Yeah, some bullshit about feeling guilty about the role he played in my being here because of the affair."

"He always was a good man," my mother replied. I laughed right in her face. Nathan had said such terrible things about my mother, and he never pretended to be able to stand her, even in her presence. She'd often told me he was driving a wedge between us, yet somehow, he was a good man now.

"What's so funny?" she quipped.

"Are you shitting me? A good man?" I questioned.

"Language, Lizzy," she warned, which was absolute insanity since I'd learned every foul word in my vocabulary from her.

"Mom, is it the fact that he cheated on me that makes him a good man or that he is engaged to another woman while he's still my husband?"

"That's not fair, Lizzy. Men stumble."

"Stumble." I nodded as I repeated the word. I wasn't surprised by her statement. After all, she had told me on my wedding day I needed to understand what a man needs. I'd known it was her way of telling me not to lose my shit when he eventually strayed from our marriage. I hated that she had been right. "He bought another fucking house for a woman where he went to start another family with her."

"I can't say what he was thinking or how he justified it to himself." Mom chose to believe the scenario my defense team put forth, which happened to be a random intruder broke in and murdered Alison. "You never know, had things turned out differently, maybe you and he could have built a life raising that baby."

I blinked at her repeatedly in confusion. "What baby? His mistress's baby?"

"Yes, if he knew how much you loved him and wanted to make it work, I'm sure he would have left her, and then who knows? Maybe that woman would have even let you two adopt the baby."

"Are you insane?" I gasped. "Do you hear yourself? You're a complete nut job. There was no intruder, Mother. It was him. Nathan murdered Alison."

"Stop, I deserve more respect than this," she warned. She hadn't abandoned me after the conviction. I supposed she did deserve some small amount of my appreciation. "And you know the police said there was no evidence linking him to the crime scene."

"His fingerprints were already there because he practically lived there part-time. There were no signs of forced entry because he owned the house."

"I don't want to go through all this again," she protested as she rolled her eyes in disgust.

"I'm not going to sit here and let you call him a good man after everything he did."

"Well, none of that changes the fact that you talking to his fiancée is simply crazy."

"Right. You suggesting I raise my husband's love child with another woman is completely normal but me talking to a woman who might be able to help get me out of here is what's crazy," I growled.

"What are you even talking about?"

"She came here because she wants me to sign divorce papers, but she can help me."

"You're not making any sense, Liz."

"I know there has to be something out there that proves Nathan did this, and she could be the person who helps me find it," I explained. "She can get close to him, look around for something that would help prove I'm innocent."

She sighed an exaggerated breath. "You have to stop this. It's not healthy."

"Think about it, Mom. Nathan is supposedly dealing with the loss of his pregnant mistress at the hands of his deranged wife, and you don't think it is even slightly odd that he's already engaged to another woman?" She seemed confused by my question.

She shrugged. "Some people use love as a way to help deal with their pain."

"You would know."

"Li—" My name fell partially from her lips before it cut off, and I immediately regretted what I'd said. The fact remained that almost everyone I'd known had abandoned me after the trial.

"I'm sorry. I shouldn't have said that."

She didn't reply, only acknowledged my apology with a slight nod of her head.

"Your sister wanted me to thank you for the postcard. She wishes she could visit, but she's just been so busy with the boys." My mother was the master at changing the subject. My sister was also a master at throwing the fact she had zero issues regarding childbearing in my face. To her, it was just one more point on her side of the scoreboard.

I wanted to tell my mom that it was all a lie. My sister never intended to visit me, and I was just fine with that. I hadn't seen her since the day of my sentencing. She had given me a stiff hug and told me to hang in there. *Hang in there?* Who the hell says that to someone who just got a life sentence? I wasn't heading off for a tough summer at camp. My life had just ended, and all she had to offer me was a hang in there.

My sister had also married up and escaped our train wreck of a childhood, and part of me couldn't blame her for wanting to protect the life she'd built. My issue with her was she had always been envious of Nathan's success. Her safe and cozy existence in middle-class America with two kids and the white picket fence wasn't enough once Nathan purchased our home in one of the most coveted zip codes. When Nathan bought me a new sports car shortly after she got her minivan, she was sure it had been an attempted insult to her. I could have told her that it was his way of trying to distract me from my latest miscarriage, but why should I? I owed her nothing.

"Lizzy?" My mom called my name.

"Huh?" I gasped as I jerked in my seat slightly.

"Are you even listening to me?"

"Sorry, I must have zoned out."

"What's going on with you?" she asked.

"Mom, don't flip out, okay?" Anytime I prefaced a conversation with this, it was almost always certain my mother would flip out.

"What?" she asked hesitantly as she flipped the postcard between her fingers.

"I'm only asking this because I'm worried she might be in trouble," I continued.

"Who might be in trouble?"

"Dr. Powell."

"Lizzy, I thought we'd settled this." Mom had a way of doing this. She would give her side of an argument, I would disagree, and she would consider the matter closed because I should do what she wanted. "You have to stop this."

"Mom, please, listen to me. She's been coming here, and she's been writing me, but the last time I saw her was the day before your last visit, and I'm worried something may have happened."

"You have to stop this. You can't go down this road again."

"What road?"

"You know what I mean."

"No, Mom, I don't. What the hell are you talking about?"

"Oh, don't act all innocent, Lizzy. You even admitted at the trial you were stalking that poor girl."

I blinked widely in shock at her words. "I think stalked is a little harsh."

"Well, what would you call it?" my mother whispered angrily.

"How about I took an interest in the woman my husband was screwing?"

"For Christ's sake, you installed cameras in the woman's house," my mother hissed.

"Language, Mother," I snipped.

"Lizzy, I'm serious."

"Okay, I fucked up. Is that what you want me to say? I took it too far. Fine, I did, and I regret everything I did, but I didn't kill that woman."

"We all know you didn't, but this is sick."

"What is?"

"Talking to Nathan's new fiancée after everything that happened."

"Why do you think she's coming here? She wants to find out the truth about him. If I can show her how evil he is, maybe she can help me find the evidence against him to get me out of this place."

"Lizzy, stop!" My Mom raised her voice before she quickly quieted it again, eyeing the guard across the room. "You think this woman is going to find evidence that the police couldn't? You don't hear how crazy that sounds?"

I waited before I spoke until I was sure she was done. "What if the police didn't find anything because they had already made up their minds?"

"She's coming here because she wants you to sign the divorce papers so she and Nathan can move on with their lives. I want the same for you, baby. Can't you see that?"

"Move on?" I repeated her words. "How exactly do I move on, Mom? He took everything from me. I'm going to be in prison for the rest of my life."

"That's not true. We have an appeal coming up. You don't know how that will go."

"You don't think that's actually going to work, do you?

Even the lawyer said it was a long shot without any new evidence."

"But it's still a shot," she insisted.

"This appeal isn't going to change anything, and you know it. The only chance I have is if they find new evidence, and Evelyn is my best shot at that."

"Stop it. You don't know that's the case."

I could see she needed the lie. My lawyers had never been shy about the fact that the evidence against me was pretty damning. I'd planted a camera in Alison's home. I'd brought a weapon as well as equipment to dismember Alison's body with me that night. My defense of "I changed my mind, and someone else must have found my stuff and committed the murder precisely as I had planned" hadn't created reasonable doubt the first time, and it certainly wouldn't be enough to grant me a new trial. I guess one positive thing in all of it was that Massachusetts didn't have the death penalty.

"Mom, hear me out for a second."

"I don't think it's healthy to keep—"

"Wait, please," I begged. "Just listen to me, for once. What if I'm right about Nathan? What if he did do this? What do you think a man capable of such things would do if he thinks his fiancée is going behind his back and conspiring against him? Dr. Powell could be in real danger. If something happened to her too, I don't think I could forgive myself."

She hesitated for a moment as she started wringing her hands anxiously. "What if . . . I mean, would it make you feel better if I told you I saw her, and she's just fine?"

My head started to throb, and I struggled to breathe as I processed my mother's words. Was that why Evelyn hadn't written me, or why she hadn't been back to see me? Had my mother destroyed my only chance at freedom? I knew when I'd sent the postcard it had been a gamble. I'd done it to myself.

"What did you do?" My eyes glassed over, and my voice shook as I spoke.

"I did exactly what you asked. I looked up this Dr. Powell and tracked her down."

"Did you speak to her?" It felt like all the oxygen was being sucked out of the room as I said the words. "I told you to keep it a secret."

"I don't know what you expected from that postcard you sent. It was so cryptic. I was trying to figure out how on earth this woman could possibly help you, as you'd said in your message."

"Mom, please, you have to tell me everything that happened. Don't leave anything out," I pleaded.

"There's not that much to tell," she continued. "I went to see her at Mass General."

"Wait, what?"

"That's where she's a doctor," my mother explained. "I assumed you knew that." I didn't know that. When Evelyn said she was a therapist, I'd assumed she worked at some private office with an oversized monstera plant in the corner of the lobby. It had never even ventured into the realm of possibility that she worked at the same hospital where I had given birth to my son.

"Why would I know that?" I snapped.

"I don't know. You're the one having regular conversations with the woman."

"What did you talk about?" I pressed.

She shook her head. "Nothing really. I told her I was your mother and that you thought she might be able to help you."

"What did she say?"

"That's when she told me she was engaged to Nathan and explained why she had come to see you in the first place."

I shook my head. "Okay, is that all?"

"Not exactly," she started. "I told her this entire thing had been very hard on you and . . ."

My stomach sank when she hesitated. "And?"

"And that I didn't think it was very healthy for the two of you to be talking, and . . . that her bosses would probably agree with me."

"You threatened her?" I nearly choked on my tongue.

"No, I simply tried to get her to see how insane this is since you are having trouble being the rational thinker in the situation."

"Mom, I can't believe you did that," I stated, but I could believe it. This was exactly like something she would do. My mother had been more than happy to rip through her children's lives like the tornado she was whenever the mood suited her. I got exactly what I deserved for sending her that postcard.

I hated that I couldn't look up anything about Evelyn, yet my life was an open book thanks to the trial and the internet. I just wanted to even the playing field a bit by learning more about her and who I was dealing with, but now it was all over. Any hope I had of Evelyn Powell helping me secure the evidence I needed to get me out of here was gone.

∼

13

I'd contemplated how to handle the revelation that my mother had spoken to Evelyn. I considered calling her at work but knew it would be hard to explain why she received a collect call from a correctional facility. A letter seemed like the best or rather the only option I'd had left.

Dear Evelyn,

First, let me say I'm so sorry. Apparently, you met my mother. Even Nathan would probably be happy to tell you she's always been a toxic person in our lives. Let me assure you, she's all bark and no bite. She has zero intentions of alerting your bosses to our conversations.

I'm not sure what else she said to you, but I hope that she's not part of the reason I haven't seen or heard from you lately. I think deep down she means well. She always seems to go about showing her love for her family in all the wrong ways.

I will admit, I was surprised when she mentioned you work at Mass General. I'm not sure why since it is such a large hospital. I was a patient of their maternal-fetal medicine program for high-risk pregnancies. In fact, I gave birth to Matthew there.

Anyway, I felt like we were starting to get somewhere in our discussions. I was looking forward to talking to you about the day I'd confirmed the affair. What I learned about the lies Nathan was living went so much beyond anything I had ever thought could be a reality.

The day I confirmed the affair, he had left early. He was gone before I had even awoken. It was something he would never have done earlier in our relationship. He couldn't stand to leave without at least kissing me first. I should have known that something was wrong when that changed, but I assumed he was giving me space. I suppose I thought I was also giving him the room he needed after losing Matthew.

It had been a couple of months since I had first seen the blonde at the company party. Despite trying my best not to think about her, for some reason, when I got up that day, I decided I needed to know. I don't know what I even thought I would do or what I was expecting to see. I suppose I just got tired of pretending everything was okay. I was sure if Nathan saw me, I wouldn't be able to undo that. I wouldn't be able to pretend I didn't know what was going on, and that would most likely mark the end of us. After all, if I forgave him, it would be like I was permitting him to do it again.

I got up and rummaged through the storage boxes in the basement until I found the brunette wig I'd worn at a Halloween costume party one year. I remember exactly how different I looked that day. I wore a dress that crossed over my body and tied at my waist. I hadn't liked how it was so revealing on me and had decided to return it, but I knew Nathan had also not seen me in it, and the dull gray color might be enough to help me fade into the background. I tied a soft blue scarf in my wig and did my makeup with deep ruby lips and oversized sunglasses. It wasn't enough. He would have spotted me in a heartbeat. I slipped the scarf out of my hair and onto my neck and instead hid my features beneath an oversized black sun hat. I looked in the mirror and hoped it was enough to conceal my identity.

I drove to Nathan's work and parked far enough away where he wouldn't see my car, and I waited. I told myself I was crazy and it had to all be a misunderstanding. He wouldn't, he couldn't betray me, not like that. Not after everything we'd been through together. The battle raged in my mind for hours until finally I saw him. He emerged from the glass doors, squinting before sliding on his shades. My heart fluttered as it often did when I would see him, but just as quickly, it sank when I saw her emerge from behind him and take her place on his arm as if it was where she naturally belonged.

I told myself they were just good friends, colleagues who worked alongside one another. I knew it wasn't the truth, but a part of me needed it to be. I told myself I was a terrible wife for not trusting him and how disappointed he would be if he caught me following him. I still followed them, though. They took her car. I wondered if he was afraid of being spotted if they were in his.

I weaved in and out of traffic, a careful ballet to avoid being seen until we arrived. Sorellina. We always went to that restaurant when there was a reason to celebrate, like anniversaries and birthdays. Nathan wasn't afraid of getting caught because the waitstaff knew us. It seemed almost like he wanted to be caught, or he didn't care. The only thing I could think of was he wanted to be free of the marriage that had become an albatross around his neck. To have a fresh start that did not include his broken wife or her damaged womb.

I couldn't help myself. I followed them in. When the hostess asked me how many, and I stated one, she suggested I sit at the bar. I took it as a good sign I wasn't recognized by any of the staff and that my disguise was doing the trick. Against my better judgment, I decided it wouldn't hurt to watch a little more. I glanced around the restaurant before I spied the pair of them in the corner booth, then made my way to the seat at the bar that would allow me to watch most inconspicuously.

What shocked me the most was the way he was so at ease with another woman. We were both flirts, we always had been, but the way we were together, I thought it was unique to the pair of us, a rare comfort. But it wasn't that I could see. At least not for him.

I nearly choked on my tongue when I placed my drink order. I could see Nathan's hand moving under their table from the corner of my eye. It moved to her leg, brushing aside her skirt as it planted itself on her knee. She didn't even seem to notice, just tossed her head back and offered an exaggerated laugh at something he said. Nathan loved it when I would laugh at his jokes.

Alison knew how to move. The way she made her blond hair fall to one side and reveal her long neck assured his eyes never strayed from her. He watched her lips as she spoke and smiled and batted her lashes at him. He wanted her. He wanted her the way he used to want me. I couldn't look away as he leaned in closer, whispering something in her ear. I wished so desperately I could know what he had whispered to her.

I can't even describe the way it felt as I watched his hand slip up her skirt and out of sight—the forbidden ecstasy on both their faces. I wanted to look away, but I couldn't. I told myself I drove him away. I deserved to witness every perverse moment of this betrayal. He pulled his hand away, licking his fingertips as she watched him, a devious grin on her perfect pouty lips. It went on and on. I ordered food I didn't eat. They ordered food they fed to one another, the entire time whispering sweet nothings.

I studied her. I recorded in my mind the way he looked at her. I wanted to see if there was a trace of that look when he saw me later that night. I hadn't been paying attention. I hadn't been looking for the changes, but I was awake now. I was wide-eyed and frozen, watching the only man I'd ever loved slip away.

Before you tell me again how you think of him as such a perfect man, please explain how he could do that to the woman he professed to love? I told myself I deserved it because of the shell of a woman I'd become since losing the baby, but funny enough, my time here in prison has helped me see I wasn't to blame. I needed him more than ever at that moment, and instead, he chose himself.

The truth is a hard thing to accept when it will throw your life into utter chaos. At least it was for me. If you are ready to hear the entire truth, I hope I will see you again.

-Liz Foster

∽

14

Evelyn had consumed my thoughts lately. I'd tried putting myself in her place, figuring out what might be going through her mind. She could claim to love him and be loyal to him as much as she wanted, but I knew she was here to make sure he was the man she thought he was before she committed to him. I felt in my gut that it wasn't just about getting me to sign the divorce papers. My job was clear after that realization. I would use her desire to be certain of her choice in partner to help her understand how dangerous he really was.

Evelyn turned her head and looked directly at me when I entered the visitors' room. She was all business again, her hair twisted up into the tight bun on the top of her head like the first time we had met. I wondered if she had come here from work or just used work as a way to fool Nathan about her whereabouts. Her pantsuit was elegant, and the simple string of pearls around her neck made me miss fashion. I missed my clothes. My mother had picked up some items from Nathan during the trial, but I never asked what happened to the rest of my belongings. I imagined him loading them into his trunk and dropping them at a donation center for the homeless as soon as the guilty verdict came back. I hoped I was wrong. My clothes were a large part of my identity, and when I got out of here, I wanted them back. I wanted everything he took from me back.

I looked at Evelyn as I approached. "I'm glad to see you're okay," I offered as I sat.

"Why wouldn't I be?" She looked at me with a confused expression.

I hesitated. I knew exactly what my response was, but I didn't want her to know I had planned out this part of our conversation. I whispered as if it were the biggest secret I had ever shared. "I was worried he would find the last letter I wrote."

She shook her head. "I've been very careful." If she trusted him so much, why would she have to be careful? She swallowed hard before she continued. "Nathan would be so hurt to read what you wrote about him."

"Well, it's the truth," I confirmed.

"There are usually two truths in any relationship." She continued to defend him, but I could see the desperation.

"What the fuck does that even mean?"

Evelyn tugged at the front of her suit jacket sleeves and stiffened her back before she continued. She looked uncomfortable in the role she had chosen for her life. "Yeah, it's horrible he cheated on you, but you said yourself you had been pushing him away."

I scoffed. "Jesus, was I as thick in the head about him as you are?"

"Excuse me?"

"Nathan had a history of screwing around long before I ever met him, but I didn't want to believe it either," I said. "You know my mom warned me, once a cheater, always a cheater. I guess that's one thing I should have listened to her about."

"I believe people can change." Evelyn had the supportive spouse script down solid, but her eyes told a different story than her lips.

People can change. Her words filled my thoughts. I'd told myself those same sentiments so many times, but now it was clear I had been lying to myself. When Nathan was in love with me, it felt like I was the only woman in the world who mattered. I learned the hard way that when you fall out of favor with Nathan, he's ruthless.

I licked my lips and warned her in as even a tone as I could. "You'd better hope so for your sake, or else maybe what you should be concerned about is once a killer, always a killer."

"This is absurd." She shook her head, clearly agitated with me. I wasn't going to get what I wanted from her if I drove her away. It would take a more delicate hand to get Evelyn to open up.

I was prepared to apologize for my last statement when she spread her hands out flat on the table. Her demeanor changed entirely, and she no longer seemed rattled. She'd had this eerie calmness about her like some switch to her emotions flipped off in her brain. If she had that ability, maybe she could survive Nathan. "I'm not going to sit here and listen to this. I don't believe he did it, and neither did the jury that convicted you."

"Ouch," I squeaked.

Her exterior remained cold and rigid. "I'm sorry, but you have to admit the evidence against you is pretty damning."

I laughed softly to myself.

"What's so funny?" Evelyn snapped.

"If I were going to kill that bitch, I would have hidden my tracks a lot better," I answered. "Don't you think it seems a little odd I wouldn't have been more careful?"

"You said in your letter you followed them to the restaurant. That's not being very careful." Evelyn settled back into her seat. She wasn't going anywhere.

"You don't go to prison for following your cheating husband and his mistress," I stated as the memory of that day in the restaurant flooded back. "You know there was one moment when I was almost certain he'd seen me. I didn't know how he could not have seen me."

"What did you do?"

"My heart was pounding so loud in my ears I couldn't hear the restaurant noise around me anymore. I thought about looking away and hiding my face, but I think a part of me wanted him to see me. I wanted him to know how much he hurt me," I explained.

"But he didn't see you?" Evelyn attempted to clarify.

"They were leaving the restaurant, and he was holding her hand. She followed him like some little puppy," I recalled before I continued my story. "He stopped at the door and looked over his shoulder at me. God, I don't know how long that look lasted. I've replayed it so many times. I was wearing a disguise, but I was his wife. That had to be why he hesitated."

"You didn't say anything?"

"A second later, they left. I tried to follow them, but after that last glance, they were gone." I sank, deflated into my seat as I recalled the pivotal moment in my life.

"What did you do?" she asked.

I pulled my lips in tight, a little embarrassed about how I'd handled the news of my husband's affair. "I went home with the plan to throw all of his things out onto the lawn and change the locks, but then I thought better of it. I knew the second I confirmed to him what I'd seen, there was no coming back from it. Our marriage would be over."

"If he was having an affair, wasn't it already over?" Evelyn posed.

I laughed and huffed as I rubbed a hand against my forehead. "Have you ever been married?"

"I haven't found the right person until now." She sounded defensive.

"I loved Nathan. He was my entire world. I'd thought at the time I had put him in an impossible position. I wouldn't let him love me after losing Matthew. I felt like I didn't deserve it. As if I'd let him down somehow. If I told him I knew about the affair and I didn't leave, it would give him the license to keep doing it."

"You don't know that," Evelyn argued. "You didn't even give him the chance to show you the type of man he could be."

"Bullshit. I've seen this story play out before. My mother put up with betrayal after betrayal. Every guy she was with would hurt her in one way or another, at least until she married my stepfather. When I got married, she told me I needed to understand how the world worked and that men had needs. I knew what she was trying to tell me, but all she was doing was justifying her pathetic excuses for relationships. If I told Nathan what I knew and didn't leave him, it would make me just like her."

"By not saying anything, weren't you still tolerating the affair?"

I frowned. "Maybe I was. You know I spent hours driving around looking for them after I left the restaurant. I checked motel parking lots for her car, drove up and down the lanes at his office, hoping they had returned to work, only to find out they had not. That was when I decided I couldn't lose him. I'd driven him into that woman's arms, and I'd do whatever it took to bring him back."

"And when you couldn't, you killed her?"

I smiled. She wanted me to say I'd done it. She needed me to admit it so she could be sure the man she was about to marry was not a murderer. But I knew that her asking the question meant she was starting to doubt his version of events.

"No, I got him back." I stood, and her eyes widened. I decided I'd had enough of Dr. Evelyn Powell for one day. Perhaps if I showed her I wasn't messing around anymore, she would show me a bit more respect the next time she came.

"What?"

"I became the woman he fell in love with," I answered. I could see from her expression she was intrigued. "I'm sorry," I said in a soft voice. "I'm not feeling well. We'll have to continue this another time."

"Liz." I heard her say my name as I walked away, but I didn't turn around. I needed her to be thinking about my story when she wasn't with me. I needed it to consume her just as my husband's infidelity had consumed me. I had to be at my bottom before seeing him for what he was. Maybe I needed to do the same for Evelyn.

∽

15

I'd spent several weeks shopping for the perfect dress for Nathan's company Christmas party, and I had found it. I'd chosen a flame-red halter gown with an intricate weaving of straps, which brought attention to the hollow at the bottom of my back. I knew Nathan loved that part of my body. He often spent a lot of time kissing it or skimming it with his fingertips. The slit up the side of the satin ensemble was high enough to make me the talk of the event.

Everything had to be perfect.

After witnessing Nathan fondling his mistress at our favorite restaurant, I'd decided I would win him back by being the picture-perfect wife. His favorite meals were prepared to perfection, waiting for him on the nights he came home. I'd traded in the frumpy sweats and house robe of a depressed grieving mother for the dresses that showed off my perky cleavage. I'd finally gone to the hair salon and had my mane returned to its former glory with some much-needed color treatment and a blowout. With every effort I made, the number of nights he made it home on time increased.

He'd noticed. That much was obvious. A kiss on my neck as he passed by. He was testing the waters. We hadn't made love since I'd lost the baby. I was not too fond of the idea of him touching me because it might lead to me becoming pregnant again. That would most likely land me right back in this place of spiraling despair when I would inevitably lose that baby as well.

Tonight was going to change everything. Tonight, I was going to reconnect with Nathan in a way that would eliminate the need for the other woman. His relationship with her wasn't one he wanted. I was confident it was one out of necessity. As soon as he knew he could have his Lizzy back, the Lizzy he had fallen in love with, he would end things with her forever.

It wasn't as if I didn't miss him touching me. I missed the way his lips felt like flames licking at my flesh as he would kiss my skin. And now, that would be possible again. Nathan didn't know I had gone to my physician and been placed back on birth control. There was no more threat of experiencing the pain that had gutted me and destroyed my marriage. I was safe to give myself to him completely. I wasn't ready to forgive him and certainly not trust him, those I thought would come with time.

"Jesus Christ." I heard Nathan moan in a low and raspy voice from the doorway of our bedroom.

"Oh hey there," I replied coyly, glancing at him briefly before returning my gaze to the mirror and slipping on the diamond earrings he had purchased for our anniversary years ago. Everything about me needed to remind him of how much he loved me if this was going to work. I even tracked down the discontinued red lipstick that he once commented on how

much he loved the shade while I was giving him a blow job. I'd thought of everything.

"You look incredible," he said as he crossed the room. I could see his eyes in the mirror were fixed on the revealing cleavage line of my dress.

I smiled, touching up my lipstick one last time, making sure I drew his attention to my mouth. "Thanks, babe," I said, trying to remain perfectly still as his hands found their way onto my shoulders. I stared up at him through our reflections.

"What's gotten into you lately?" he asked as he skimmed my shoulders and upper arms with his fingertips.

"What do you mean?" I asked, but I knew exactly what he meant. I'd been a shell of the woman I was after we lost our baby. Holding Matthew in my arms, watching him take his last breath, helpless to do anything, it broke me. It broke me in a way I didn't think I would ever actually come back from, but this was about survival. The survival of the last thing I had in my life that I loved. Nathan. My marriage. I was not going to let that go without a fight.

"Don't get me wrong. I love it," he noted as I stood and turned to face him. "I don't understand what changed. Is it the therapy?"

"I think so," I lied. I hadn't been going to therapy for a while.

He lifted his hands to my face and cupped my cheeks. "I can see a difference." I could hear the excitement in his voice.

A part of me wanted to explain that a couple of months ago, I had confirmed he was cheating on me. That he had hurt me more than anyone in my life had ever hurt me, but if I had any shot of winning Nathan back, those were details he could never know.

"Thank you for convincing me to go to therapy in the first place," I said. "I'm sorry if I've been a nightmare to live with." His hands dropped to my hips. He didn't let go of me. He liked having me close. His gaze turned away from my face, and I knew why. It was guilt. My stomach twisted as the image of him fondling that whore filled my thoughts. I started to pull away, but he tightened his grasp on my hips and pulled me in closer to him.

"Don't ever apologize for that." He was looking in my eyes again. "I'm sorry I've been such a shitty husband."

"You haven't," I lied again. He was a shitty husband. He'd betrayed me. Could I forgive him for that? Could I play house and ignore the fact that the man I should be able to trust more than anyone wasn't worthy of that trust?

I fought the urge to ask him how he could jeopardize everything we had built to be with her. I'd already played through all the responses he might come back with in my mind. She meant nothing, to which I would reply that was even worse because he had risked it all for something meaningless. The one response I was the most afraid of was telling me he loved her. That it had meant something and he had to follow his heart and be with the woman he now loved. No. I would not reveal that I knew his dirty little secret. Instead, I would have to learn how to live with the information I now possessed.

He moved in close and began kissing my chin gently. Questions started to race through my mind. Did he use condoms when he was with her? Did he tell her he loved her? Did he tell her I was just an obstacle in the way of their happiness? I pressed my eyes closed and tried to focus on him. His lips, his touch, he was here with me, not with her. I was *winning him back. Once he saw I could be the wife he'd once loved, I would never have to think about her again. I just needed to keep this up a bit longer.*

But it wasn't just a bit longer. I would need to keep Nathan's secret to myself for the rest of my life. I would need to pretend what he had done didn't break me for the rest of my life, or it was clear I would find myself right back in the same spot I was in now. Despite everything in my core screaming that this relationship was not worth repairing, I couldn't let him go. Nathan was the only man I'd ever loved. He was the only man I ever wanted to love.

I pulled away, trying not to reveal what I was keeping buried just below the surface.

"Liz, what's wrong?" *Nathan knew me better than anyone. It would not be easy to hide things from him. Then I realized, maybe he could redeem himself. What if he told me about the affair himself? If he came to me, begged for my forgiveness, it wouldn't mean I was weak. It would clarify to him that I wasn't willing to be treated in such a way ever again but I loved him enough to work on us. The trick would be getting him to tell me.*

I broke free from his grasp and collapsed onto the bed. "Nothing."

"Please, Liz, we were finally getting somewhere. Tell me what's going on in that head of yours."

"Do you still love me?" *I asked in a whisper.*

"Of course I do. How could you ask me that?" *he replied quickly.*

"I haven't made it easy on you," *I continued.* "You were going through the same pain I was, and I was so cold to you."

"I know that wasn't you."

"Nobody would have blamed you if you'd left." I tossed the bait out delicately at first.

He chuckled as if the idea were preposterous. "Leave you? You can't get rid of me that easily."

No, he hadn't left me. What he had done was far worse. "Thank you." I forced the words, my voice cracking.

He looked away from me for a moment, and there it was again, the guilt I needed him to show if I had any hope of him confessing what he had done. "You're my wife. There's nothing to thank me for."

"I see now how unbearable I've been," I continued.

"This isn't productive, Liz. Beating ourselves up for the things we've done or haven't done isn't going to help us move past this in our marriage," he stated firmly as he took a seat on the bed next to me.

I tossed one leg up and over his legs. I allowed the deep slit of my dress to expose my long and lean leg, the panel of fabric falling to rest between my legs. "I don't know what I would do if I lost you," I said as I cupped his cheek with my palm and stared into his eyes.

"I fucked up," he revealed at last. This was it. He loved me enough to tell me everything he did wrong.

"What do you mean?" I gently prodded.

"I mean, I haven't been the husband you needed me to be, and for that, I'm so sorry." Jesus Christ, Nathan, enough with the vagueness.

"What do you mean you haven't been the husband I needed? You've stood by me faithfully during all of this." There, let the bastard not confess with that statement hanging out there.

He shook his head and turned his body into mine, causing

me to fall back onto the bed, my legs naturally parting around him. "I'm going to be better. No more working late," he started. You mean no more going to fuck her after work. "I'll come home for lunch a couple of times a week," he added.

He pressed his lips against mine, and I let my arms rest around his neck, my nails entangling in the base of his hairline. He pulled away. "I need you to tell me you forgive me, Liz."

"Forgive you for what?" I pressed, waiting for him to finally be honest with what had been going on.

"For being an idiot," he gasped, and I felt his body shake on top of me. "I can't lose you."

If I pushed anymore, I ran the risk of him becoming suspicious of what I knew. "There's nothing to forgive," I stated, making sure he would not feel absolved from his sins.

His mouth found mine again, and I melted into his kiss. He wasn't ready to confess, and I wasn't prepared to forgive him. That was going to take a bit more time and some more coaxing.

His hand ran up my exposed leg before it slipped between my legs. He pulled back slightly, a smirk planted firmly on his face. "No panties?" he growled with one cocked brow.

"You wouldn't want me to have panty lines, would you?" I flirted. I knew it wouldn't take much to light Nathan's passion. After all, we'd never had an issue in the bedroom before Matthew. He'd been respectful of the time I needed after it all happened, but it had been too long. It had been the length of time it takes for a marriage to be on life support.

"That would be unthinkable, especially in this gorgeous gown," he said as I wiggled one shoulder and caused a strap to

fall, revealing my breast. He wasted no time taking my bare nipple into his mouth.

I moaned when I felt him slip his fingers inside me. It hadn't been only Nathan that missed the connection between us. The way he stroked and moved with my body, I felt like an instrument he played a beautiful song on. I pressed down on his fingers as they moved deeper inside me.

"Fuck I've missed you," Nathan muttered before placing my nipple back into his mouth. My dress was half off. He made quick work of unbuckling his pants. When I'd thought this evening out, I had planned to give him the most fantastic blow job of his life, but it was clear he needed to be inside me as much as I needed him to be.

Before I had time to suck in another breath, he slipped himself in, and we both let out a moan of delight. It felt right when we were connected this way, like two puzzle pieces that finally connected.

He shifted his position to hover over me. "I love you," he confessed as he gazed into my eyes.

"I love you too," I admitted. I wasn't sure I could ever trust him again, but I knew I would be lying if I said I didn't love Nathan.

My hips started to buck wildly as he pressed deeper into me, the rhythm of our motions coaxing me to come.

"Jesus, I missed how fucking wet you get," he said with a hot breath against my ear before he moved his mouth back to mine and began to kiss me with even more pressure, penetrating my mouth with his tongue. I tried to block out the intruding questions. Did she get as wet as I did? Were there things about her he enjoyed more than with me?

I wanted him to be inside every part of me at that

moment, to melt into him and let the world fall away. I never want to think again about dead babies or mistresses. Our lives had grown too complicated, too damaged, and I wanted desperately, if just for a moment, to have back what we had been.

I knew it was a lie, but I was fine pretending, even if it was just for one night.

His movements were as skillful as they had ever been. At that moment, I'd won my husband back. It might have been temporary, but it was what I needed to keep fighting. There was nothing he wanted more in the world than to please me. Once again, I was the object he worshiped.

He lifted my chin and forced me to look into his eyes. "Do you want to come with me?"

I shook at his words and opened my mouth to answer him, but nothing came out.

I tried desperately to reply, but suddenly, I felt him starting to slip away. The bed disappeared from under me, and I was falling into blackness. I attempted to shout his name, but still, there was only silence. The blanket of darkness enveloped me as I continued to fall, helpless to stop it.

Just as suddenly as I had started to fall, I awoke, and a strangled breath escaped my throat. I panted and wanted to scream. I trembled as for a moment, the breath of Nathan in my unconscious mind still lingered on my flesh. I was desperate to figure out how to purge him from my mind forever.

"Fuck you, Nathan," I whispered as tears gathered in the corners of my eyes. I wished I had never met him.

16

When I entered the room, I spotted Evelyn looking out the window. I waited for her to notice me, but she didn't immediately, lost somewhere between her mind and what was on the other side of the window.

I had only met with Evelyn a handful of times, yet something about her felt like I'd known her for years. I felt comfortable sharing with her. Perhaps it was the fact she was a therapist, and she was skilled at disarming people. Something told me that wasn't it, though. She seemed vulnerable when I spoke to her. I wasn't sure if that was a good thing or not.

Anxiety had surfaced inside me that I might have been putting this woman in danger. I'd played a role in Alison's death, and I would have to live with that, but was I putting Evelyn in the same danger? I'd seen what Nathan was capable of. What would he do if he felt betrayed by Evelyn? My fears didn't change that she was the only one close enough to Nathan to find the evidence to free me.

"Is everything all right?" I asked as I approached.

Her head jerked as if I had pulled her out of a trance. Her eyes widened when she looked at me, and she smiled as she returned to reality. Something felt different about her today. She'd been so calm and collected in all our previous meetings. This Evelyn felt disheveled. She kept looking around her as if she were worried someone was watching her. "Sorry, I'm a bit out of it today," she offered with nervous laughter.

"Are you sure you're okay?" I asked again as I took a seat.

"I said everything's fine." She raised her voice slightly before correcting herself. "Don't be silly."

Something was different. Something had her rattled. I wondered if it was Nathan. Were my fears valid? Was he starting to figure out what she was up to?

"What happened after you followed him to the restaurant?" she asked, not allowing me the opportunity to probe further.

"What?"

"Last week, you were talking about how you followed him to the restaurant. You said you got him back. What did you mean by that?" The conversation came flooding back. I saw Evelyn's hand trembling. It looked as though she might jump out of her skin.

"What is going on with you?"

She shook her head, and when she did, I noticed the dark circles under her eyes. "I don't know what you mean."

"You look like you haven't slept in days," I stated.

She forced a brief smile before she dismissed my suggestion. "I told you, I'm fine. I had an emergency call from a client last night and then had too much coffee to compensate this morning." She waved a hand in my direction as if she were physically waving off the concern. "The last time I was here, you said that you had gotten Nathan back. What did you mean by that?"

I hesitated before deciding to continue with my story. "Well, I guess I should go back to the day I'd spotted him at the restaurant that first time. Nathan got home late that night, and unlike he normally did, he didn't call. I started to think that maybe he had seen me at the restaurant, and he wasn't coming home. God, that was one of the longest nights of my life."

"I can imagine," she offered.

"He was so late that it reached the point where it would have been strange if I hadn't checked in to make sure he was okay. I drove myself crazy trying to figure out what I should do," I recalled.

"So what happened?"

"Well, eventually, the decision was made for me when I heard his keys in the lock downstairs. In a panic, I jumped into bed, and I pretended to be asleep." I chuckled as I recalled the anguish I'd felt that night. "God, it seems so ridiculous now. If I could do it over again, I would have just talked to him. I would tell him what I had witnessed and let the chips fall where they may. I was scared, though, so instead, I lay there, trying not to cry as I listened to him turn the shower on in the guest bathroom to wash away the evidence of the night he'd had with her."

"That must have been so hard." Evelyn's voice was heavy with sympathy.

I sighed a heavy breath as I tried not to allow the tidal wave of emotions from that night to overwhelm me. "It was a long night for sure, but it had given me time to think. During that time, waiting for him, I decided for certain I wanted to save my marriage. I knew it wouldn't be easy, but I was determined to do whatever it took to get him back. I was awake for hours after he finally came to bed, lying there with my eyes closed. I couldn't stop thinking of the two of them together. The next morning, I got up early and made breakfast."

"You did? I don't know how you did it."

I nodded. "But he was heading out the door before I could even finish making it. I chased after him and told him we needed to talk. I begged him. He must have felt sorry for me, or maybe it was guilt, but whatever the motivation, he sat down at the dining table. I could tell he didn't want to be there because he was constantly checking his watch."

"What did you say?" Evelyn asked, her eyes fixed on me.

"I told him that I was sorry," I replied.

"You were what?" Evelyn nearly choked on her words.

I lifted a hand and motioned for her patience as I explained. "You have to understand part of me was sorry. I was sorry I had allowed my marriage to reach the point where he felt like he needed to leave our marriage to find what he needed. I couldn't tell him that part, of course, but I explained to him that I knew after we lost Matthew I'd been a terrible wife, and I wanted things to be better."

"He was cheating on you, and you apologized?" Evelyn seemed genuinely surprised.

I nodded. "An apology can be a handy tool in a woman's arsenal."

"I'm not sure I could have done the same if I were in your shoes," she admitted.

"If you had been through as much as Nathan and I had been through, I think you would find the strength. Our infertility journey stitched us together in ways that are hard to explain to someone who hasn't been there. We had been by each other's side at our absolute lowest," I explained.

She shook her head. "Sometimes, it amazes me how strong you are." My chest fluttered at her statement. She admired a quality in me. Was Evelyn starting to see that I wasn't a killer?

"He seemed genuinely touched," I continued. "He told me we'd go away and spend the weekend together. He wasn't checking his watch after that. Instead, he was confessing how he still loved me and he was afraid I no longer loved him."

"Wow." She blinked repeatedly. "I had no idea you two were trying to rekindle your marriage."

"Honestly, it wasn't at all how I expected him to react," I confessed. "It gave me hope that maybe there was a chance we could put his indiscretion out of our minds. I tried to convince myself that was the end of it, and I had my husband back."

"But you didn't?" Evelyn searched for the rest of the story.

"This was the period I was only privy to what I experienced. I don't know what he told Alison, but we didn't go away that weekend. It did happen, but it was several weeks later, after his company Christmas party." The dream I'd had the night before of the first time we'd made love after I discovered the affair filled my thought, but I pushed the mental images aside, deciding there was no need to share that detail with Evelyn.

"Was he still seeing her during that time?" she inquired.

I shook my head. "I don't know. Looking back, I'd say probably. At the moment, I told myself it was over."

"You didn't have any lingering suspicions?"

"You have to understand. Nathan was very convincing. The weekend he took me away was perfect. It felt like when we had first gotten married. That's when he asked me if I wanted to try for another baby."

"He what?" She seemed surprised by this revelation.

I nodded. "I let myself be vulnerable, and I told him I was scared, and he assured me we could adopt and he would be just as happy. I think I always knew he wanted a child of his own, some twisted, fucked-up thing to make his piece-of-shit father happy. I mean, he never accepted his son, so how would he have treated an adopted grandchild?"

"I haven't met him," Evelyn interjected.

"Who, Nathan's father?" I laughed. "I can count on one hand the number of times I saw Nathan's father, so don't feel slighted."

"He sounds terrible."

"He wasn't an available father figure to Nathan. Who knows, maybe that contributed to why he's as fucked up as he is." Evelyn winced at my suggestion.

"What happened next?" she asked, and I could tell she was trying to change the subject from Nathan's dark side.

"I couldn't tell Nathan, but I wasn't ready to start trying to have another baby. I needed to have my husband back for a while before I figured out the family part," I continued. "I didn't tell him I'd gone back on the pill."

She looked confused. "So he thought you two were trying to have a baby again?"

I nodded. "Nathan wanted a family. He'd always been driven to find that thing he had been missing in his childhood."

She shook her head. "So he had been having an affair and then all of a sudden decided he wanted to try starting a family again."

I smiled and nodded as I saw the absurdity of Nathan's logic was settling over Evelyn.

"Since his mother had been the mistress, I find it very surprising he would carry on the way he did with Alison," she said, and I could see she was sorting through the conflicting images of Nathan in her mind.

"I wondered if that was what made Nathan snap," I started. I'd had a lot of time to think about what could have driven Nathan to do what he did. "He wanted a family more than anything, but he wanted what he viewed as the family he never had. I think when he found out Alison was pregnant, he realized he was just like his father. He was going to have a child who would never be accepted in his circles."

"That's ridiculous," Evelyn gasped.

"For Nathan, who lived the life of the outcast, it wouldn't have been ridiculous," I argued.

Evelyn gripped the edge of the table, and she suddenly seemed very pale. "Are you okay?" I asked, reaching a hand out across the table. "Should I get someone?"

She repeatedly blinked as she steadied herself. She sighed. "No, I'll be fine."

"Are you sure?" I asked, concerned.

"Yeah, I just haven't been feeling well," she confessed.

"Are you sure everything's okay?"

She nodded. "I think I just need to lie down."

"Evelyn." When I said her name, she looked up into my eyes. "Are you sure you're okay? It's not Nathan, is it?"

She shook her head as her brows stitched together in confusion. "What do you mean?"

"Does he know you're coming here?"

"Of course not," she replied, shifting a hand down to her stomach. "I just don't feel well. I must have caught a bug from the hospital or something. I should go."

"There's so much more I need to tell you," I added, hoping I could encourage her to stay.

She stood and turned toward the door. "I'm sorry, Liz. I have to go. I'll be back, though."

As I watched Evelyn walk out the door, I lingered, hoping she would reconsider and return. She hadn't looked well. I just hoped it was a bug, as she claimed, and not something more sinister. If Nathan had discovered her visits, I wouldn't put it past him to do something to prevent her from coming to see me. She didn't turn around, though, and I couldn't chase after her. I would have to do the only thing one could do in my position, and that was wait.

∼

17

"You look like you've seen a ghost," Ruby said as she sat next to me on the bench in the recreation yard.

"Huh?" I muttered, not making eye contact with her as I silently dissected my recent conversation with Evelyn.

"Yo, anybody home?" she yelled as she tapped me on the top of my head.

I shook my head and forced a laugh as I smiled at her. "Yeah, sorry. I guess I have a lot on my mind."

"You hear something on your appeal?" she inquired.

"Yeah, right." I scoffed as I lifted my eyebrows. "No, just thinking about that woman who has been coming to see me."

"What about her?"

I stared at two women as they spotted one another lifting weights a short distance in front of me. "She came to see me yesterday, and something didn't feel right."

"What does that mean?" Ruby inquired as she started

to shift the dirt in front of us with the heel of one of her shoes.

I shook my head. "She didn't look well. She was pale, and she seemed distracted. She ended up leaving because she said she felt sick."

"Maybe she was sick because she realized what a ho she's being," Ruby suggested.

"Stop it," I replied with a smirk. "She seems pretty nice the more I've gotten to know her."

"You're too nice," Ruby huffed.

"I'm just worried maybe Nathan is behind whatever is going on with her."

"Like what, he poisoned her or some shit?" Ruby asked.

My stomach twisted as that thought hadn't even entered my mind. "Well, Jesus, I hope not." I gasped. "She said he still doesn't know she's coming here."

Ruby tilted her head. "I mean, he's got to be one crazy asshole if he's gonna poison his latest girlfriend after all the shit that went down around him."

"I mean, I guess you're right," I admitted. Ruby had a point. Nathan was smart and careful. There was a reason I was the one behind bars and not him.

"Maybe she just realized she shouldn't be coming around here," Ruby suggested.

"Not you too," I growled. "I hear enough of that shit from my mother."

"You should be hearing it from everyone. It's not normal to be talking to that woman. She doesn't have your best interests at heart," Ruby warned.

"I don't know what else I'm supposed to do," I said,

touched by how protective she was of me. "My appeal isn't going anywhere if they don't find some new evidence. Evelyn is the person closest to Nathan. If anyone could find something, it would be her."

Ruby started to fidget and shift in her seat uncomfortably.

"What is it?" I asked, knowing she had something to say.

"You mean it when you say you didn't do this?"

"Do what? Kill that woman?" I exclaimed in surprise. "Jesus, no, I told you I didn't."

"Please." Ruby chuckled. "Everyone in this place says they didn't do it. I'm supposed to think you're somehow different?"

"All this time, you thought I could do something like that?" I felt sick as I asked the question.

"I don't know. After the shit your man did to you, I'm not sure how I'd react," Ruby admitted.

I rolled my eyes. "Well, I know you well enough to know that you wouldn't do something as terrible as go murdering a pregnant woman."

"You said you thought about it," Ruby reminded me.

"Yeah, well, thinking about it and then actually doing it are two different things." And they were. It was like I was allowing one of the crime novels I loved to play out in my head. I never really wanted to kill Alison. At least, I didn't think I did.

She huffed. "Fine, whatever. I was gonna say that Marla might be able to help."

My head snapped in her direction. "What on earth could she do?"

"She knows people on the outside who might be able to figure this out for you," Ruby replied.

"Like lawyers?"

Ruby laughed. "No, not lawyers."

I shook my head. "I don't think I need the kind of help you're talking about."

"No, hear me out," Ruby protested. "I mean, she wouldn't do it for free or nothing, but if you think your old man is hiding something, she knows people who will get him to tell them what you want," Ruby said in a whispered tone.

"I wouldn't even know what they're looking for," I admitted.

"Trust me, they'll get him to talk as long as they get paid."

"Ruby, stop," I commanded in a firm voice. She looked at me in surprise.

"What? Marla likes you. I'm sure she'd do it if you asked."

"No, I don't want her to," I snapped.

"Geez, you don't have to get so bent outta shape." Ruby huffed. "I was just trying to help."

I took a deep breath and calmed myself before I apologized. "I'm sorry, I know you were. I'm getting close with Evelyn. I can feel it. I just have to keep on her."

"If you say so," Ruby replied.

∼

18

I stepped into the visitation room, relieved when I saw Evelyn had returned.

"What happened to you last week? Are you okay?" I asked, taking my seat at the table she was already seated at.

"I'm so embarrassed," she answered. "I'm afraid I must have eaten something that bothered me." I could tell she was lying.

"Are you feeling better?"

"Much." She forced a smile. "Where were we before I ran out of here?" She giggled awkwardly as if to try to lighten the mood around her sudden exit the week before. It was clear she wasn't going to give any hint as to what had actually caused her emergency exit.

"Let me see . . ." I started as I tapped a finger on the surface of the table.

"You thought the two of you were starting to work on things," Evelyn offered.

"Oh right," I said as I snapped my fingers. "He was still working late sometimes, but I told myself that it was normal and we were good, so I needed to trust him. Then it happened."

"What happened?" Evelyn inquired, watching my mouth, desperate for the words they possessed.

Our eyes linked, and I thought how strange it was that her eyes were brown. They were beautiful, like deep mahogany, but my eyes were a glacial blue. Alison's eyes had been blue as well. All of Nathan's ex-girlfriends I'd met had blue eyes, and for the most part, they had been blondes. Evelyn wasn't Nathan's type. Maybe that was the point. Perhaps a woman who was his type would remind him too much of everything he had done to the women he had claimed to love.

"I went to his favorite bakery to pick up a cake for his birthday, and when I went inside, I saw her—the woman from the restaurant and his office. Since I'd been with him at company events, I knew she would recognize me if she caught sight of me, so I watched from the corner of the room, careful to conceal myself behind the other customers. Then I saw them lift the lid to a cake for her approval. It read 'Happy Birthday, Lover.' Who the fuck actually calls someone lover on a birthday cake?"

Evelyn snickered. "Someone most people would hate."

"Exactly," I said, feeling vindicated.

"So he was still seeing her?" Evelyn asked.

"I told myself it wasn't what it seemed and the woman was desperate and probably just trying to convince him to come back to her. I watched her as she left and climbed into a BMW. I don't know what made me do it, but I decided to follow her, so I abandoned my place in line, ran out, and jumped in my car."

"Did she see you?"

I shook my head. "No. I have to admit it felt exhilarating. I felt like a character in some spy novel."

"I bet."

"Anyway," I continued, "I followed her across town to a newer neighborhood. I wasn't super familiar with the area, but I knew there had been a lot of development around there. She parked and walked up the drive of a cute modern new construction home. I'd imagined her in some pink stucco apartment building with leopard fabric chairs, so it surprised me when I saw such a quaint home."

"What did you do next?" Evelyn asked. Those big brown eyes suddenly seemed so desperate.

"I probably should have headed home, but I couldn't help myself. I decided I needed to find out her name. At that point, I had no idea who she was other than the blonde from Nathan's work," I explained. "I don't know why. I guess I just thought if I knew her name, it would somehow unmask her and take all of her power away. I'm sure that sounds crazy."

Evelyn shook her head. "Not at all. A lot of times, the unknown is the scariest of all."

I shook my head as old regret settled over me. "If I'd just gone home and pretended I never saw her, maybe things would have turned out differently."

"Did you confront her?" Evelyn asked.

I laughed at the suggestion. "God no. I looked up the property records on the county website to figure out her name. Only the owner wasn't her. it was a business name," I recalled. "I recognized it immediately. E and N Properties." My voice cracked when I recalled the memory.

"Are you okay?"

I nodded and took a breath. "Yeah, sorry, it was really hard to see that name. It's the investment company Nathan started for rental properties we owned. It stood for Elizabeth and Nathan Properties."

"Wait, what?" Evelyn shook her head in confusion. "Nathan owned that house too?"

I nodded. "We owned that property. Nathan had his girlfriend living in a house that he bought with a business in our name. That was when I knew this wasn't some office fling. He cared about her, enough that he was paying for the home she lived in."

"Liz, I'm so sorry, that's awful." I could see in Evelyn's expression that she was sincere. She was starting to see the cruelty in the man she loved. "What did you do?"

"Honestly, I don't remember what I did at that exact moment. I started driving around, and the next thing I knew, hours had passed, and I was sitting in front of my house."

"What do you mean hours passed?" Evelyn questioned my statement.

"I don't remember." What I hadn't told Evelyn was I got migraines, and sometimes, on bad days, I wouldn't remember things that happened. "That day is a blur." I forced a laugh.

Her brows narrowed. "I don't understand, so you don't remember anything that happened after you figured out who the house belonged to?" I no longer felt like Evelyn was a growing ally. Instead, I suddenly had the overwhelming sensation I was under a microscope.

"Yeah, I guess." I huffed.

"Does that happen a lot?" Evelyn asked, her eyes uncomfortably fixed on me.

"I know what you're doing," I blurted out defensively.

"What do you mean?"

"You're trying to make me think I'm crazy," I hissed.

"Liz, no, I'm not. I'm worried about you." Evelyn's voice was tender, but I could see through to her true motives.

"Yeah, sure you are," I snapped. "I'm not an idiot. Nathan used to do the same thing to me all the time."

Evelyn took a deep breath, and it was clear she measured her words carefully. "Losing time can be a symptom of some pretty serious medical conditions."

"I'm not sick, do you understand me?" I realized I had started to raise my voice when I saw the guard behind Evelyn shift her gaze to focus on me.

"I'm sorry, I wasn't trying to upset you," she offered.

"I'm not upset," I insisted, embarrassed by my reaction. I bit at my bottom lip, my face hot with frustration, before I asked. "Where was I?"

"You had just figured out that Nathan owned her house."

I repeatedly blinked as I straightened out the wrinkles in my gray scrub top. "Oh, yes, that's right," I said, clearing my throat before I continued. I avoided looking Evelyn in the eyes, not wanting to see what might be reflected of me in them. "I texted Nathan to ask when he'd be home. I told him I had something planned for his birthday. I figured if it was really over between them, he would have made sure to make it home. I told myself it had to be a misunderstanding."

"And was it?" I looked at her, eyes wide. "A misunderstanding?" she clarified.

"He said he had to work late."

A moment of silence lingered between us as the impact of his lie settled over the quietness. "I'm sorry."

"God, I look back on that, and I'm so embarrassed."

"Liz, you didn't do anything to be embarrassed about. He was the one who was cheating." I laughed slightly at hearing her defend me and condemning Nathan. "What is it?"

I shook my head as I continued. "I begged him, I told him we needed that night, and I'd make sure he wouldn't regret it. Jesus, I was so pathetic. I was practically hysterical. He said he was sorry, but he couldn't. At first, I was pissed, but then I ended up texting him a dozen times, asking him when he would be home. I can imagine Alison and him having a good old laugh about Nathan's pathetic wife."

"I'm sorry," she whispered. "That must have been terrible for you."

"I was the woman who no longer got to spend her husband's actual birthday with him. I got it the day after. I felt like I'd become the mistress," I added.

For a second, it looked like Evelyn was going to reach

out and touch my arm, but then she thought better of it. "What happened after that?" she pressed on.

"I could tell I was losing him, so I told him I understood," I replied. "And then I drove back to her house and made sure I parked far enough away that nobody would notice my car, and I waited. I waited until my husband arrived and walked into their home. Their home." I repeated the words. "They had a life together I wasn't a part of."

"Didn't you want to confront him?"

"Of course I did!" I exclaimed. "But that's a bell that can't be un-rung. I couldn't imagine a life without Nathan. I'd been out of college for ten years at that point, and I hadn't had a real job the entire time. What on earth would have become of me?"

"You're strong Liz, I'm sure you could have figured something out," Evelyn offered.

"I didn't want to figure something out. I wanted my life back." The dread I'd felt that night as I saw everything slipping away from me crept back into the pit of my stomach. "I always wondered what men told the other woman. Do they tell them they're just looking for a way to leave? Do they say they've been miserable for a long time? Or does the other woman not even care? Is she just happy to get him for any portion of time she can? Nathan seemed like he was happy when he was with me like he wanted to restart our lives together, but there he was, blowing out the candles on her lover cake."

I glanced at the clock, realizing Evelyn's visiting time was almost over. She was too focused on my story to notice. As I shared the events of that night, I could see Evelyn was repulsed by what her beloved was capable of.

"Wait," she interjected. "If her name wasn't on the property, how did you find out her name?"

I started to laugh.

"What?" She begged, "Tell me."

I bit at my bottom lip before I revealed. "I stole her mail."

Evelyn chuckled. "I guess that was a pretty simple way to do it."

"I also tossed the mail in the trash, which included the statement for her car payment." I smiled as I recalled the childish moment of spite. "And it felt good." The mail had been a normal and rational response that any wife would have had. I could retell that without the shame that came along with the story of how I had planned to kill the woman.

Evelyn's attention shifted to the people around us as they started to stand and make their way to the exit.

"Oh gosh, what time is it?" I didn't reply. "I leave tomorrow for a work trip, but I'll be back next week, okay?"

I nodded. My story with Nathan was starting to come to an end. If I didn't convince Evelyn to help me soon, I may never.

"Evelyn." I called out her name as she started to walk away. She paused and looked back at me. "I didn't kill her."

She offered me a tight-lipped smile and nodded in my direction. "I'll see you next week."

Was her nod an acknowledgment? Did she believe

me? Was there a chance this was actually going to work? The questions raced through my mind as my heart started to pound in my chest.

"Foster!" the guard exclaimed. I looked around to realize I was the last one seated. "Move it!" I hopped up and hurried past the guard.

∽

19

"I hear you need a friend on the outside," Marla said as she moved in next to me on the walking track.

"What?" I asked, despite already knowing what she was talking about. Ruby had done the exact opposite of what I'd asked of her.

"What kind of help are you looking for?" Marla inquired as she glanced around to ensure nobody was close enough to hear our conversation.

"You misheard," I replied as I cleared my throat and quickened my pace. "I'm not looking for any help."

"Oh, come on, don't be such a baby. Nobody would be able to trace it back to you," she assured me in a dismissive tone.

I shook my head. "Look, I appreciate the offer, but this is all a big misunderstanding."

"Oh, so you did kill that woman?" she asked, and I was surprised momentarily by the abruptness of the question.

"Well . . . no, I didn't."

"So if you don't need any help? I guess that means you're okay rotting away in here for something you didn't do?" she pressed.

"I've got it taken care of."

"Does that mean you don't think your husband did it anymore?" Marla asked pointedly with her heavy Boston accent.

I stammered as I tried to find the correct response. "No . . . I-I mean, well yes, I think he did."

"You think? Either he did it, and he's why you're here, or he didn't."

"I don't know!" I exclaimed as panic welled inside me.

"Look, all I'm saying is I have some friends who could have a chat with him and get to the bottom of things real quick," she said. "By the time they finished, you wouldn't have any doubts whether or not he did it."

"No, you can't."

"You're just going to let that piece of shit get away with it, aren't you?" Marla asked, but she didn't wait for me to reply. "My husband thought he could do whatever he wanted without consequences. I knew about his side pieces. What he didn't realize is I didn't give a fuck. But when one of those young things convinced him she would make a better partner in the family business than me, well, that's when I had to stand up for what was mine."

"I'm sorry, that sounds terrible, but it's not the same thing," I insisted.

She looked at me and grinned. "Sure, it's not. I didn't let the piece of shit get away with it, and you shouldn't either."

"I appreciate what you're trying to do for me," I started.

"Us women gotta look out for one another." I tried not to laugh when she said this, considering I'd witnessed Marla slamming another female inmate in the face repeatedly with her lunch tray, breaking her nose in the process, earlier that week. I knew help from Marla would not come from the goodness of her heart. She would expect some favor or payment in return. I also knew if Marla helped me, as she called it, there was a pretty good chance Nathan would end up in the hospital, or worse.

"I completely agree," I said as I treaded further into the conversation with caution. "But I think I've almost got it figured out. If some guys go and rough Nathan up, there's no way the person I need to help me will ever trust me."

Marla scratched her head. "I thought you were smarter than that."

I sucked in a large breath of air and tried my best to sound calm and collected. "I know what I'm doing."

"That girl ain't ever gonna roll on your man."

"You don't know that," I snapped.

"Would you have?"

I stopped walking when she asked me the question. If someone had presented me with hard proof that Nathan did something terrible, would I have protected him? I wasn't sure I could answer the question in the way I wanted to. I loved him. I loved the life we had together. I would have done anything to protect it, so much so that at one point, I even contemplated killing someone.

"I don't know, but I have to hope maybe she's a better person than I am," I said at last in an almost whisper.

Marla reached out and gave my arm a gentle squeeze. When our eyes connected, her gaze was empathetic, and I thought it was the kindest act I'd ever witnessed from her. "Come see me when you realize it won't work."

20

I entered and searched the visiting room with my eyes. I looked back at the guard who had escorted me inside when I didn't recognize anyone, but she had already redirected her attention elsewhere. I turned my head back to the room of people and examined the faces at each table one by one.

My breath caught in my throat as my gaze settled on a woman sitting alone with a hat pulled down on her lowered head. There was a sinking feeling in the pit of my stomach when she looked up, and our eyes connected.

"Brook," the name escaped my lips as I crossed the room to stand in front of my sister. "What the hell are you doing here?" The words fell out of my mouth before I even had a moment to process what I was saying.

"Gee, nice to see you too, sis," she snarled, and I quickly remembered all the reasons I'd loathed her for most of our lives.

One of the guards furrowed her brow at me, and I quickly sat down at the table across from my sister. "Are you fucking kidding me right now?" I nearly choked on my tongue as I spat the words at her. "Not so much as a single word from you since the trial, and then you show up here acting like I'm the bitch? How exactly were you expecting me to react?"

Brook stiffened as she smoothed out her long blond hair that stuck out from the bottom of her cap. She pulled on the hem of her soft pink polo shirt to remove any wrinkles and cleared her throat but didn't immediately speak. She had an agenda. I was sure of it. Brook wouldn't risk someone seeing her visit her convict sister otherwise.

"I can't just want to check in on you?"

"No," I snapped without hesitation. I knew Brook. I knew she was born without an ounce of empathy and she'd been jealous of me from the moment Mom brought me home from the hospital. There was zero doubt in my mind that she wanted something.

"Why do you always have to be like this?" she asked in a strangled whisper as she glanced around at the tables on either side of us to see if anyone was watching our interaction.

I laughed. "Really? Are you worried someone you know might see you here? Don't worry, Brook, I think your secret about your crazy sister is safe."

"I never said you were crazy," she protested. "You're always putting words in my mouth."

"Oh my God, just stop it and tell me why you're here." I huffed.

She sucked in a deep breath and then slowly released it. She closed her eyes as if she were trying to calm herself. I'd thought many times throughout my life that they must have switched one of us at the hospital. We were nothing alike, and I could never remember a time when we got along.

"I know you're angry." She started at last as I waited for her to reveal why she was there. "And I know that you still want to hurt Nathan for what he did, but you have to think about what you're doing. Do you realize how it's affecting Mom?"

I repeatedly blinked in confusion. "What are you even talking about?"

"Nathan. I know you blame him for your being in here," she continued.

"Umm yeah, that's because he's the one who murdered someone," I bit out.

Brook rolled her eyes. "I'm not going to sit here and go through this with you."

I knew what she meant by that statement. Brook never thought I was innocent. She'd always thought I'd killed Alison, or at least deep down hoped I had. Then that would mean she was the golden child and not me. I inhaled sharply. "Great, then why are you here?" I asked again, deciding any other conversation with her would be fruitless.

"I think you know why I'm here," she added in her condescending tone.

"Jesus, I wouldn't have asked if I knew."

"This business with Nathan's new fiancée," Brook whispered.

"Oh, my God," I grunted as I shifted back in my seat. "I take it you've been talking to Mom?"

"Not just Mom."

My head tilted as I looked at her with a focused glare. Had she also spoken to Evelyn? I felt like I had no control over any aspect of my life. I was here, locked away, and life was proceeding to move forward outside of these walls. Even things that affected me, I had no control over, and I found it infuriating.

"Do you know how hard it must have been for him to reach out to me?" Brook asked, and with those words, my head started to spin. I felt the earth shift under me, and I gripped the edge of the table to steady myself. I stared at her, but despite my mouth desperately wanting to say something, words escaped me.

"He just wants all of this to be over," she continued. "We all do. I know he hurt you, and honestly, I agree he's a real piece of—well, you know what, for putting you through what he did. But don't you think he's been punished enough?"

"Punished enough—" The words came out of me as a squeak.

"Yes, honestly, it's a miracle he even found someone else after . . . after everything." When she said those words, she looked away from me. There it was again. Brook's way of letting me know I was the cause of everything terrible that happened in the world and how much better life would be if I weren't a part of it.

"Nathan knows? He knows about Evelyn's visits?" I managed at last as I ignored my sister's insinuation. When the reality of what Brook was telling me set in, panic washed over me. If Nathan knew that Evelyn was coming to see me, he would be outraged. She wouldn't be safe. Anyone he felt was a threat to him would be in danger. What if he thought she was helping me figure out how to prove my innocence? What would he do since my innocence would only reveal his guilt?

Brook shook her head in disgust. "Listen to you. You say her name like she's your friend or something. She's not your friend, Lizzy."

"Shut up, Brook, you don't know what you're talking about. Does Evelyn know that he knows?" I asked, my voice revealing my desperation and fear.

Another eye roll from Brook. "How should I know?"

"Brook, listen to me," I pleaded. It was the first time I had ever asked anything from my sister. I reached out and touched her arm across the table. "You have to go and check on her, make sure she's okay."

She pulled away, and a disgusted look planted itself squarely on her face, which was an achievement in itself, considering how much she'd had in Botox injections. "I will do no such thing," she gasped. "This madness has to stop; do you understand me? If not for your sake, then Mom's."

"What are you even talking about?" I growled. "What the fuck does any of this have to do with Mom?"

"That's so like you." She started. "You never think about how your actions affect other people. Well, you're killing her. Do you realize that?"

I was the one rolling my eyes after that statement. My mother was always the queen of manipulation, and it appeared she was still working her magic on my sister. "Are you serious with this shit?"

"I knew it was pointless to come here," she huffed as she tossed a hand into the air. "A complete waste of time."

"Brook, wait," I said as I looked into my sister's eyes, hoping by some miracle I might be able to convince her of the gravity of the situation. "Please, no matter what you think of me or what you think I did, will you just check on Dr. Powell?"

My sister stood. Apparently, she had decided our conversation was over.

"Brook?" I called after her as I watched her move away, helpless to stop her.

She turned and met my desperate gaze. "No, I'm not going to check on her." Her tone was steely. "This is for your own good. And I know you're not going to listen to me because you never have before, but you need to stop contacting her. This has gotten out of control."

"I know you don't believe me, but he's a monster." My voice cracked as I begged.

She stiffened. "He might be, but a jury found you guilty. Why don't you do everyone a favor and let us all move on with our lives?"

∽

21

It had been two weeks with nothing—no calls or visits from anyone in my life. I'd reached out to my lawyer in a desperate attempt to have someone check on Evelyn but was informed by a not so friendly paralegal in their office that was not something they did. Evelyn had told me she had a business trip but that she would be back the following week. That date had come and gone with no word, and as another week ticked by, my fear that something had happened to her grew.

In desperation, I decided a letter was once again my best and only option.

Dear Evelyn,

I hope this letter finds you well. After a recent visit from a family member, I discovered you and I may not be the only ones aware of our visits. You can imagine how concerned I was after learning of this information.

Please understand the danger this may put you in, and it's of the utmost importance you exercise extreme caution based on this. I know you don't want to believe me, but he's capable of so much more than you could ever imagine.

Even if you do not want to continue with our conversations, I would greatly appreciate it if you could just let me know that you're okay. The last thing I would ever want is to do anything that would contribute to putting you in harm's way.

Sincerely,

Liz

This was too private for a postcard. Instead, I folded the paper into three and slipped it into an envelope. All I could do was send it and wait. Send it and hope I wasn't too late.

∽

22

My name was on the list that day. I had a visitor coming to see me. I knew my sister wouldn't be back anytime soon. I thought it could have been my mother, but it did seem too soon for her as well. I hoped it was Evelyn. Besides being worried for her safety, it had been nearly three weeks since we last spoke. I actually missed her.

Since Evelyn's absence, I was having trouble sleeping. My appetite was nonexistent, and the headaches and dizzy spells I'd struggled with after we lost the baby had returned and were becoming more frequent. I'd planned to see the prison doctor, but of course, I hadn't mustered up the courage to go.

"Liz," the guard said my name, and I looked up at the unfamiliar face. She was new, and there was an innocence and sympathy in her eyes when I looked at her. I'd thought to myself how this place would undoubtedly cause her to lose that. She motioned for me to come to the entrance of the room.

I was instantly filled with relief when I saw Evelyn. She sat on the far side of the room at a table in the corner. She was dressed in an emerald satin top and cream-colored slacks. A large billowy bow was tied at her neck, and her hair was slicked back into the familiar tight bun.

I approached her slowly, waiting for her to make eye contact with me. When she did, I smiled, unsure what kind of greeting I'd receive from her.

"Did you get my letter?" I asked.

She nodded. "I did."

"He knows," I blurted out, unable to conceal my concern.

Her reply had shocked me more than anything else she could have said. "I know, we talked about it." She was so calm as she said the words matter-of-factly.

"What?" If they had talked about it, there was no way he would have allowed her to come back here. Unless . . . what if she had ended things with him? She wouldn't be able to help me if that were the case. She would be safe, though. I looked at her hand. No. The ring was still there.

"He was upset at first, but he understands why I had to do what I did."

"Evelyn, you can't trust him," I pleaded. If he acted as calm and reasonable as she claimed, I found that even more concerning. I never saw it coming. Nathan pretended that everything in our life was wonderful while engaging in a secret second life.

"I know." No, I was wrong. There was one other thing she could have said that would have shocked me more, and that was it.

"Wait, what? I don't understand—" I felt a knot in my throat, and my eyes grew wet. "You believe me?"

"I didn't say that," she clarified and then hesitated a moment before she continued. "Honestly, I don't know what I believe. Nathan has been acting strange ever since he figured out what we've been doing. I told him I needed to come to see you one last time."

"One last time?" My heart sank at her words as I repeated them.

She looked away from me as if it were too hard for her to say the words while seeing the desperation in my eyes. "Look, Liz, I'm sorry you're in here. I'll admit, it's hard for me to believe that you did what they say you did, but I can't keep doing this. At one point, I thought about leaving and never seeing either of you again."

"You did?" I asked, hopeful. "Is there a chance that's because you know who he really is?"

"I said I'd thought about it, but then I remembered why I came here in the first place and the man who I believe him to be. I can't keep doing this. He's going to be my husband," she explained.

"You're still going to marry him even though you don't believe him?"

"I didn't say I didn't believe him." Her tone became defensive before softening slightly. "I said he was acting strange, but honestly, what man wouldn't act weird if their fiancée was speaking to their soon-to-be ex who murdered their mistress. God, it sounds so crazy when I say it out loud." She shook her head. "I'm sorry, I didn't mean it like that, but you have to understand where I'm coming from."

"Where you're coming from?" The desperation was gone, and now there was nothing but contempt in my voice. "If you're okay marrying someone who would do the things he's done, then fine, maybe you deserve everything that's coming to you."

"I'm sorry, I wish it didn't have to be like this," she offered.

"You're such an idiot! Can't you see he's manipulating you? He manipulates everyone! Jesus, you wouldn't believe all the lies he told her about me."

"What? Told who about you?" Evelyn asked, confused.

"Alison. The things he told Alison." I rolled my eyes. "I'm sure he's told you the same lies."

"What are you talking about?" She looked back at me, still seemingly confused.

"Please, I'm not stupid."

"I honestly have no idea what you're talking about," Evelyn continued to defend herself.

"I know what the jury thought when they saw the tapes I had from inside Alison's home. They listened to all those lies he told her about how I was unhinged and that he was worried about what I was capable of."

"Nathan has never said anything remotely like that about you to me," Evelyn replied.

"I don't believe you," I said forcefully. "I watched what he said to Alison. He loves to portray me as crazy. He knew exactly how it would make me look when the jury saw those tapes."

"You mean the tapes that only existed because of the

cameras you hid in her home? Do you even hear how you sound?"

"You're like all the rest of them, twisting what I say."

"Did you put those cameras in her house?" she asked pointedly.

I stiffened. "You have to realize how hurt I was when I found out what he'd been doing. When I'd thought he'd ended it only to discover it was still going on right under my nose. I also was smart enough to know what kinds of things Nathan could be opening our lives up to with what he was doing. I was protecting him."

Evelyn shook her head. "I don't understand. How on earth were you protecting him?"

I sighed, annoyed nobody could seem to grasp why I needed to keep an eye on Alison. "I knew if Nathan wasn't careful, someone like Alison could exploit us."

"So you're saying Alison was what, blackmailing Nathan?"

I shook my head. "I don't know, maybe. It was clear she had some sort of power over him."

"Well, the way Nathan tells it, you two were over, and he was worried that you were so distraught over losing Matthew that if he ended things, he wasn't sure what you might do," Evelyn said sharply.

"He's lying!" I hissed. "We weren't over. Nathan wanted to try to start a family with me. I knew he'd eventually grow tired of her, and when he did, I wasn't about to let her ruin everything we'd built."

"So you killed her?"

"Stop it. you're doing it again, twisting everything I

say. You're trying to get me to say I did something that I didn't do."

"Isn't it more believable you put cameras in her house because you were consumed by jealousy?" Evelyn no longer felt like an ally. I felt the burning of her judgmental eyes on my flesh.

"You have no idea what you're talking about." I hesitated. My heart started to ache at the memories of what I'd witnessed in the footage from Alison's home. To know your husband is screwing around is one thing, but to see it on a screen was something completely different, but I had done it to myself. Put myself through the pain of watching it all.

Evelyn's eyes widened. "You have to admit it makes more sense that you couldn't stand the idea that he was with another woman than it being some elaborate plan of Nathan's to frame you. After all you were the one who was watching them and you were the one who had planned to kill her."

"He loved me. I knew some fling wouldn't change that."

"So what, he loved you so much that you think he framed you for murder?" I felt my guards go up with her continued badgering.

I sat quietly for a moment before I asked. "You said you met Nathan at a grief counseling meeting, is that right?"

Her head tilted as she flashed a puzzled expression. "Yes, why?"

"Was this before or after my trial?"

She lifted her brows. "Excuse me, what are you trying

to say?"

"Just answer the question," I urged.

"After, he was there because he said he felt like he'd lost everyone in his life he ever loved," she replied, and my chest deflated. What had I become? "So what, now you think I'm somehow involved?"

"I'm sorry." I shook my head, and my voice cracked as I found myself on the verge of breaking down into tears. "I don't know what else to do."

"What does that mean?"

"I didn't do this," I stated. "I know I didn't, but that doesn't seem to matter to anyone. Nobody will help me." I felt the warmth of tears as my eyes glassed over.

She half-chuckled. "You know part of me still wants to believe you. I've been through this a million times, it just adds up that it was you, but for some reason, I don't believe it."

"Because it wasn't."

"Well, I also don't think it was Nathan either," she declared. "Why are you so against the idea that it could have been a home intruder?"

"It's impossible. There would be too many coincidences," I argued. "I tossed the knife I'd brought with me into the trash at a park when I decided I couldn't go through with it, but that was the same one used to kill Alison. The cameras were also in the bag I tossed. I know I got rid of all of it, but the knife was used to kill her, and somehow, the bloody knife made it back into that bag I had tossed. It had to be him. It's the only reasonable explanation."

"Is there any chance that maybe Alison found you at

her house, and you two got into an argument, and then things got out of control?"

"What? God no!" I exclaimed.

"Are you sure? I don't think anyone would blame you for not wanting to remember something so painful. Is there a chance you blocked it out of your mind?"

"I think I would remember butchering some poor girl." I gasped, wondering if she could see on my face that part of me feared this could have been exactly what happened. It hadn't escaped me how bad the evidence against me looked. Any reasonable person would have questioned their own sanity at some point, but I couldn't believe I wouldn't have remembered ending Alison's life.

"It's not unheard of for people to block traumatic events away in their subconscious," she suggested in a gentle voice.

"Stop it!" I exclaimed, standing. "I'm not going to sit here and keep defending myself over and over again. I didn't do it!" She peered back at me with surprised eyes. "You need to leave."

"I didn't mean—" I didn't want to hear anything else Dr. Evelyn Powell had to say.

"Now," I commanded.

She stood and appeared to be waiting for me to stop her. When I didn't, she moved toward the exit.

"Good luck," I called after her in a steely tone. "I hope things go better with him for you than they did for me." I watched Dr. Powell leave the room for what I assumed would be the last time.

23

Dear Evelyn,

I stared at the name I'd written on the piece of paper. I must have gone back and forth a dozen times, debating if the letter was a mistake. I'd lost my temper. I'd blown my one chance at finding someone who might actually be able to help me get out of this place. When it looked like Evelyn had started to conclude I was likely behind Alison's murder, I couldn't stop myself from lashing out because it felt like the trial all over again. The way she looked at me reminded me of the way members of the jury had looked at me. The truth was, though, if I was going to have any chance of getting out of here, I needed to win her to my side. I needed to show her what the jury couldn't see. I did not kill Alison.

I'm sorry. Those words seem like the only possible way I can start this letter.

I hope you will allow me the chance to explain. I understand if you don't ever want to come back, but I hope you will read this letter in its entirety. If you're still considering marrying Nathan, you should know what happened the night of Alison's death.

I knew there was a chance that no matter what I said, Evelyn was done, and I would most likely never see her again. While it was a gamble for me to write down in a letter what happened on that night, I didn't see how I had any other options.

I will admit that in my lowest of times, I'd thought the only way I could see Nathan not straying again was for me to remove the temptation of Alison altogether. Maybe it sounds like an excuse, and perhaps in a way it is, but planning how to rid our lives of her gave me something to focus on. Something that could consume my thoughts and prevent me from actually hurting someone or myself. Looking back, I realize it was a mistake and something I wish I had never been a part of.

I did hide the cameras in her home. I think I was fooling myself when I convinced myself I was doing it to protect Nathan. Being in prison has a way of forcing clarity, and I realize, no matter what I try to tell myself, the truth is I needed to see how strong their relationship was. To see if he could ever love me again. It broke me when I saw the way he looked at her. It reminded me of the way he'd always looked at me.

I wish I could tell you all I did was hide the cameras, but unfortunately, what I witnessed only fueled my desperation. I'd decided there was only one possible solution. I know how it must make me look, but I started researching ways to kill someone and dispose of the body. At first, dreaming about Alison's murder was enough, but I quickly needed more. I needed a concrete plan to tell myself I wasn't allowing this woman to steal my life as I sat idly by. And so that's when I started to purchase supplies.

I looked at the words as I wrote them. I was ashamed of what I'd allowed myself to become, what I'd allowed Nathan's betrayal to do to me. I was just as much to blame in everything that had happened.

Something started to change, though. Just creating the plan empowered me. Suddenly, I was beginning to take a little bit of my life back. It wasn't overnight, but I was becoming the person I used to be. Looking back, I think that was the point Nathan found my surveillance equipment. This was when I think he turned the tables on me and hatched the plan to set me up for the murder of Alison.

I felt my body clench as I penned the words. The revelation that I had been in her house and I had gone there to kill her made my chest ache. I felt like I couldn't recognize the woman I had been at that point in my life. She seemed like a stranger to me.

But my newfound strength wasn't enough to see me through what I saw on the video that set that night into motion. Alison revealed to Nathan that she was pregnant, and something in me snapped. It hadn't been enough that she took my husband. She was going to have the family with him we had tried for years to have. Suddenly, the plan I never thought I would ever act on felt like it was my only option. I remember going to her house thinking I was finally going to end this. But that's not what happened. I promise.

I got there before Alison came home, and when I saw the ultrasound picture on Alison's dresser, I came to my senses. I couldn't believe what I was about to do. I was scared I'd let it get as far as I did. When I looked at that ultrasound, it was like an eye-opener for me. It was at that moment when I decided I was going to go home and confront Nathan. I would tell him I still loved him, and if he wanted to stay married to me, he would need to end things with Alison. He could be a father to their child, but she was not part of the deal. If he didn't want a life with me, I'd decided I would have to let him go.

After leaving that night, I stopped at the park and tossed the equipment I'd brought with me into the trash. When I finally returned home, I found Nathan was in the shower. I was so emotionally drained by everything that evening I decided to wait until morning to talk with him.

I remember sitting across from Nathan the next day, trying to decide how to start the conversation. I knew he'd be furious I'd been spying on him. I just kept waiting to say something until later that evening. There was a knock on the door. It was the police. They wanted to talk to him at the precinct.

When he returned from the police station, he sat me down and told me about the affair and that the woman had been murdered. By then, it was too late to tell him everything that had happened. I didn't speak. What could I say? It was impossible. I'd planned this woman's demise, but I didn't do it. I couldn't tell him anything because I knew exactly how it would look.

Instead, I watched as he wept, begged for my forgiveness, and then I got to watch him as he struggled with his grief. He was honest about it. He told me he loved me, but he also loved her, and he promised me we'd get through it. He was so convincing.

The next time the police knocked on the door, they weren't there for Nathan. They arrested me. I was so confused and scared. They told me they had received an anonymous tip about where the hunting knife used to kill Alison had been purchased. They pulled the store's security footage, and that's when they saw a clear image of me.

The tip could have only come from Nathan. He was the only one who knew about Alison and the only one who could have figured out what I was planning. I had been so isolated during that time and hadn't told anyone about Alison, even those closest to me. The man you're planning to marry murdered the woman carrying his child, and he framed his wife for it. What do you think he would do to you if he ever perceived you as a threat?

Liz

My hands trembled as I sealed the words into the envelope and sent them out into the world. I couldn't be certain what the result would be. Would those words change Evelyn's mind? Would the next time I heard from her be that she was going to help me?

24

My heart pounded so hard I couldn't hear any other sounds in the room. My brain was screaming silently at my feet, telling them to turn and run, but they refused to move. My mouth went instantly dry, and it felt like the walls were shrinking inward on me.

He was seated at the table where Evelyn usually awaited me. When our eyes met, I thought he looked as anxious as I did.

His hair was longer than I'd ever seen it. It brushed against the collar of his shirt, and he had grown a beard. He looked different. No longer like my Nathan, but somehow still exactly like him.

I sank my teeth into my bottom lip, willing myself to move forward. I walked to the table where he sat. The table I'd expected to see Evelyn sitting at. Evelyn. Where was she? Had he gotten my letter instead of her? Had he had enough of her betrayal?

I ran my hand down the front of my clothes as if

somehow straightening out the fabric would make the prison uniform look more presentable. My hands moved up to my hair that hadn't had a proper cut in well over a year. I tucked the ragged pieces that framed my face behind my ears. I felt nauseous but tried my best not to reveal to him what his presence had done to me.

When we were married, Nathan loved to surprise me. *When we were married.* I considered the statement silently in my mind as we stared, each one waiting for the other to speak. Weren't we still married?

Why was he here? He didn't appear angry as he looked at me. He seemed . . . sad. Was he sad? Was he sad because of what he'd done to me? Did he regret it? Why did I feel like it mattered if he regretted it?

"You look nice." The words left my mouth before I had even realized what happened.

He stiffened immediately, and the sadness I'd thought I had seen was gone, replaced with the contempt I had seen in the courtroom.

"This isn't a social visit," he replied in a stern tone. Of course, I knew he wasn't here on a social visit. He had not come to see me a single time since my arrest. He'd gotten his way. I was behind bars, and he would never have to deal with me again. But then, why was he there?

A sour taste filled my mouth, and I felt like I might be sick. A million questions had gone through my mind since I'd found myself in this place that I wanted to ask him. At that moment, though, I couldn't verbalize a single one. Instead, I just stared at him, eyes wide.

He shook his head. "A part of me doesn't blame you. I can't imagine the pain you went through, the pain I put you through." I couldn't believe my ears. Was he admitting that he was behind everything? My palms started to sweat—a desperate satisfaction overtaking me. Even if nobody else would hear his confession, it was unimaginable to have him finally validate that I wasn't crazy.

He swallowed hard before he continued. "For that, I'm sorry. I know I apologized when I first told you about Alison. The affair was inexcusable. It all spiraled out of control so quickly . . . but what you did, Lizzy, what you took from me." He sighed. "I never imagined that was possible, especially by you."

I straightened my back and repeatedly blinked as I processed what he was saying. "What I took?" I repeated the words in confusion.

"I get the hurt and the outrage, and I take full responsibility for the part I played. Jesus, that's all I thought about during the trial. What if I'd never gone on that first lunch with Alison? What if I'd ended our marriage before I ever pursued someone else?"

"Ended our marriage?" I yelped. The reality that Nathan had considered ending our marriage settled over me. I loved him, but I'd gotten it all wrong. He had cared about me, there was no denying that, but did he ever love me like I thought he had?

"After our son, though . . . what you did, it's unforgivable," he continued, and my head started to throb. He hadn't been admitting anything except the affair. It wasn't a confession. It was him confronting the person he thought murdered the woman who was carrying his unborn child.

My breath stuck in my throat. He viewed me as that

person. It didn't make sense. He did it. I was already behind bars, so why continue with the charade?

I thought of the empty nursery in our home. The wallpaper mural Nathan had so painstakingly helped me hang. I'd wanted to hire out the task, but he said it would be fun to prepare the baby's room together. If things had turned out differently, he would have been such an amazing father.

I was terrified of becoming a mother. I never thought I wanted kids. After my controlling and manipulative mother, I was scared to grow up and become another version of her. Nathan convinced me I could never be anything like her, and our family would be cherished.

After we were married, we'd joke with each other that our five-bedroom home wouldn't be big enough to hold the family we'd planned to have. But then, with each negative pregnancy test or miscarriage, the reality of our situation sank in. It was life's irony to hand me the curse of a broken womb only after I decided I wanted to have children.

"Evelyn cares about me, and I think I can make her happy." His words broke through my thoughts. Evelyn. He acknowledged her existence.

"Make her happy. Does she make you happy?" I asked, wishing I didn't want to know the answer.

He sighed and looked down at his hands that were folded on the table in front of him. They didn't look like the hands of someone who could stab someone to death. I wondered if I would have recognized hands that I thought were capable of such a crime. I hadn't seen my husband as a man capable of living a double life until he already was. Maybe I wasn't good at seeing what people were truly capable of.

"I don't know if I deserve to be happy, but I guess she gets me as close as I'll probably ever be able to get again," Nathan replied. I stared at his eyes. The corners of one of them trembled as they turned glassy. The sadness was back. "I don't think I would have made it through all of this without her help. I had some pretty dark nights where I thought—" He shook his head as if he were shaking off a nightmare before he cleared his throat and continued. "What matters is that she loves me, and she deserves to be happy. She's a good person."

"I was a good person," I replied.

"Maybe at one time we both were good people, but look at the lives we've destroyed," he said. "I want you to stop talking to Ev."

Ev. It felt weird to hear him use a more casual version of her name. Was that the name he used when he would come home? Would he call out Ev into the emptiness, searching for her? When he called her to say he would be late, was that the name he used?

"She's the one who came to see me," I reminded him.

"She thought she was helping me," he answered. "I know you hate me, but don't you think you've punished me enough?"

"You ruined my life, Nathan," I snapped.

"I was unfaithful, Lizzy. Lots of men are unfaithful. Their wives don't go murdering their mistresses," he snapped right back.

"I didn't murder anyone." My voice cracked as I defended myself. "And you know it."

He clenched his hands into two tight balls on top of the table, and I watched as his knuckles turned white, the tension of his frustration rippling up his forearms. He sucked in a sharp breath, then continued. "I told myself when I came here I wasn't going to do this with you."

"Do what?"

"Let you suck me into your delusions."

"I'm already in here. You won," I spat the words at him. "There's no need to keep up with the lies."

"I thought maybe you'd get the help that you need in here."

"Help that I need?" I growled as rage welled up inside me. "How's it feel? Are you happy with yourself? Maybe the reason you're so angry with me is because I can see through all your bullshit lies."

"Whatever you say," he huffed dismissively.

"What, are you worried that Dr. Powell is going to start seeing you for the monster you are too? 'Cause she will. I can tell I'm already starting to get through to her."

Nathan leaned forward as he briefly glanced around the room and lowered his tone. "This has to stop. I fucked up, okay? Is that what you want to hear? I'm sorry. Jesus, you have no idea how sorry I am. But Alison didn't deserve what you . . ." His voice cracked, and he hesitated for a moment as he pulled his arms in close and crossed them over his chest as if to place a protective cocoon around himself. "Nobody deserves to have done to them what you did to her."

I opened my mouth to speak, but nothing came out. *What I did to her.* His words repeated themselves over and over again in my mind. There was no reason for Nathan to lie anymore. A jury found me guilty. Nobody believed me, and if he admitted his guilt, there would be nothing for him to lose. Nobody would still believe me, but I could see it in his eyes. He wasn't lying.

When he was with Alison and would lie to me, he would always do it over the phone. Or he'd find a way to be walking into the other room so that he was never looking at me when he spun his webs of deceit. At that moment, though, Nathan was looking directly at me. There was no averting his gaze to try to protect his mistruths. When he looked at me, he believed he was looking at a murderer.

My mind started to spin. Could it be true? Had I been wrong all this time? Was Nathan not responsible for the death of Alison? It didn't make sense. If it wasn't him, who could it have been? Alison was killed using the items I purchased in the way that I had planned. Who could have known what I was planning? It couldn't have been a coincidence. Someone had to be following me that night and see me toss the bag into the trash at the park. I'd purposely chosen to dispose of the bag at that park because I knew it was dimly lit and there were no cameras. Nobody would have seen me. But obviously, someone had. Someone had to call that tip into the police about where I had purchased the knife.

Unless . . . As I sorted through the possibilities in my mind of what happened that night, I was snapped back into reality when Nathan stood. He looked pointedly at me and said, "If you ever loved me, please, just leave us alone." He turned and walked away, and I would have called after him, begged him to talk more with me, but I was too consumed with the realization that my assumptions all this time had been wrong.

The police found the bag in the trash can I had used. The cameras were inside. I'd put them there. When the police found it, though, everything inside was covered in blood. Everything I had brought to the scene with me, including the murder weapon, was inside, but when I tossed the bag in the trash can, there wasn't blood on any of it. It didn't make sense.

I came to my senses that night when I held the ultrasound picture. *What if I hadn't changed my mind that night? What if I ditched the bag after . . . after . . . No! I couldn't have.* I screamed inside my head. *I left. Didn't I?* My head had started to swim with confusion when I'd felt the guard's hand on my arm. Nathan was gone, and I was left with so many more questions than I'd had before he came.

∼

25

I could still hear Nathan's voice as he told me how hurt he was by what I took from him. The way he looked right into my eyes and told me his version of what happened. The pain on his face revealed that he believed I'd killed Alison and his unborn child.

There had been zero doubt in my mind until the moment he sat across from me. I was confident it had been him. After all, we had never actually discussed what happened that night. After I was arrested, everything became about my defense and talking to the lawyers.

At that point, I hadn't pieced together the events that ultimately led me to conclude Nathan was the killer. Anytime I had seen him in the courtroom, he had seemed so depressed. I remembered I'd felt sorry for him. I'd thought how hard it must have been for him to watch his wife on trial for murder. Later, I'd decided it had all been an act. But what if it wasn't?

I pushed the library cart down through the shelves,

randomly tossing books in instead of my usual heavily curated selections. I recalled the time I'd once found the courage to speak to Alison. I'd gone to Nathan's office with the plan to walk right up to her and tell her he was my husband, and if she didn't back off, I would go above Nathan and make sure she never worked in that town again. I'd planned out my entire speech to her and even practiced it in the mirror.

"I was once the other woman," I'd said to my reflection. "And had I known that at the time, I would have turned Nathan's advances away. You know he's married, which makes what you're doing despicable. You should be ashamed of yourself, preying on a man who's grieving over a lost child.

"I'm here to let you know that I know. If you do the right thing, maybe I won't say anything, and maybe you'll be able to keep your job. Did you know he still makes love to me? He still tells me how he wants us to have a family. You're a distraction. I'm the love of his life. He will never leave me for you, no matter what he says. When all this is over, your life will be destroyed, and I'll still be married to the man I love."

I'd had several versions. I wanted to make sure it was perfect before I approached her because I wanted zero hesitation in my voice. I never said any of those things, though. I went in the morning to talk to her because I knew Nathan would be in meetings. I looked amazing. I made sure of it. I wore a pink, playful A-line skirt trimmed in satin. To accentuate my chest, I chose a cross-body-wrapped shirt that was respectable while it also gave the nod to my ample cleavage.

I'd taken a deep breath as I exited the elevator that day and walked with such sure strides. Chills ran up and down my spine as I crossed the office floor, clutching my small purse. I felt powerful, as though I was there to take back my life, and nobody was going to stop me.

I'd caught Alison in my sights. She looked amazing as well, which did cause my pace to slow a bit. As she whipped her head to the side, it was like her hair moved in slow motion, and suddenly, I realized I wasn't moving at all anymore. I couldn't just turn around. I'd already come too far. People had seen me and would notice if I tried to leave.

As I'd stood there in the middle of Nathan's workplace, I felt the pressure as it started to build behind my eyes. A migraine was coming on. I darted to the left and rushed into the bathroom, sorting through my purse for my prescription painkillers.

Just when I thought I'd mustered the strength to slink out of the bathroom and hurry back to the elevators, Alison walked in. I could see instantly she was surprised to see me. There was also recognition in her eyes. She'd known exactly who I was as soon as our eyes connected. She also could see I'd been crying.

"Are you okay?" she asked me in a sweet soft voice. That was the first time I'd heard her voice up close. It was disarming in a way. High-pitched but tender, I imagined it would have been the perfect voice for a kindergarten teacher.

I hesitated, and she moved in closer. Reaching out, she touched my arm. I wondered if this was how it started with Nathan. Was he sad after the loss of our child? Did he need consoling I couldn't offer him because of my state? Was Alison's gentle touch what he needed to bring him back from the depths of despair? I think in a weird, perverse way, part of *me was grateful she'd been there for the man I loved when I couldn't be. How could I tell her, though, that now her work was done? She needed to let Nathan and me heal our marriage.*

I cleared my throat. "I'm fine," I'd lied, but it didn't cause her to release my arm, and I didn't pull away. I wanted to see where it was going, how this temptress had charmed my husband.

My breathing slowed, and I tried to quiet my thoughts to alleviate the throbbing in my head. "If you don't mind me saying so, you don't seem very fine," she'd stated.

I shook my head, trying to think of an excuse for my tears. "It's really no big deal. I have a migraine. I get them all the time."

"Oh no, that's terrible. My sister gets those, and they can land her on her back for a week." She had a sister. She had a family who loved her. Hell, maybe my husband loved her too. I tried to remember the words I'd rehearsed, but they escaped me as I looked at Alison's reflection in the bathroom mirror.

"Is there anything I can get for you?" The way her eyes widened and her brow stitched together, I could tell she was genuinely concerned. She'd recognized me when she had come into the bathroom. I knew it. But she hadn't seemed worried her secret would be discovered. If I hadn't seen the two of them together with my own eyes, I would have never suspected this woman was having an affair with my husband.

"I'll be fine. I just took some pain relievers." Then it hit me. I knew one way I could force a reaction. "I should probably get to my husband's office. I don't want him to worry. He's always going on and on about how worried he gets about me."

I waited for her to ask me who my husband was, but she didn't. "Oh, okay," she'd chimed in a chipper voice.

"It's crazy how worried Nathan gets about me," I added, making sure if she had any doubt of who my husband might be.

She offered a tight-lipped smile. "I'm sure he does." At that point, she released my arm and stepped into the bathroom stall and secured the door. My face had flushed hot. I wanted to shout my entire rehearsed speech at the door.

I didn't. I went to Nathan's office, sat on his couch, and waited patiently, trying to make sure another round of tears didn't sneak up on me. He didn't seem to be annoyed I was there, more puzzled. He didn't look panicked, and he didn't glance out the door to see if Alison was looking. She thought she had me fooled, but I wasn't going to let her steal my husband.

I leaned into the cart as a blinding pain shot behind my eyes and I tried to push the memory that was invading my thoughts away. The migraines had started to get worse. They'd miraculously disappeared sometime during the trial, and I had hoped perhaps I was cured. It was evident I had been wrong.

My mind pulled back to the memory of the important day. It was important because it was the day I had decided I had had enough of being played the fool. That was the day I'd first hatched the plan to take Nathan back. I'd seen how cool she was in my presence. She was a snake, and I was sure Nathan was in over his head. That was the day I'd purchased the cameras.

"Fuck," I muttered as I fell to my knees. My stomach twisted in pain as nausea from the flare of the migraine overwhelmed me. My temples started to throb, and I squeezed my eyes closed. I felt the room begin to shift under me. In an instant, I was falling, and darkness clouded around my vision until everything was silent and dark.

∽

26

"Elizabeth, are you with us?" an unfamiliar voice asked.

I groaned and clutched my head as I tried to sit up. Eventually, I gave up and collapsed back onto the bed. Above me, an older woman in a white lab coat hovered as she placed a hand on my shoulder.

"Whoa, don't try to get up, okay? We don't want another instance like the one in the library." She smiled, and it made me feel uncomfortable.

I didn't try to fight her. I closed my eyes, shutting out the brightness of the lights in the room. My head was still throbbing. I reached a hand up and felt a bandage on my forehead.

"What happened?" I questioned.

"I'm Dr. Weber. From what I was told, it sounds like you passed out and hit your head on one of the shelves in the library." I looked at her, not shielding my confusion as I noticed a guard standing near the door, watching the interaction.

Panic gripped my chest.

"I don't understand," I replied, my voice cracking from my dry throat.

"Did someone do this to you?" she asked me.

"What? No."

"You're safe now. It's okay," the woman in the white lab coat said as she attempted a calming voice. "Did you have a disagreement with one of the other inmates?" she asked as she glanced over at the guard.

"What?" The question came out with a laugh. "Are you kidding me?"

"It's my job to make sure everyone feels safe inside these walls."

"I had a migraine, that's it." I huffed.

"How often do you get these migraines?" the doctor asked as she looked at the machine that displayed my vitals. She was an older Korean woman, and I thought how slight she looked in comparison to the guard who stood in the doorway. The lines around her mouth and eyes were deep and cavernous, but her eyes looked younger than the story her face told.

I shrugged. "I don't know. I used to get them a lot, but then they went away for a while."

Dr. Weber pulled out a flashlight and shined it in my eyes, one at a time. "And do you always black out when you have a migraine?"

I considered her question. I'd never told anyone about my blackouts, not even Nathan. The blackouts and losing time had increased in frequency. I assumed they were linked to my medication since I'd stopped taking them after my arrest, and shortly after that, the migraines stopped. If that were the case, though, it didn't make sense why they had started again.

I shook my head. "No, not always, maybe a couple of times." I lied. I knew it had been more, but for some reason, I felt protective of that information.

I tried to think of the last time I had blacked out from one of my migraines. I felt queasy again when I remember it had been the night that Alison died. I snuck into Alison's place before she got home and removed the camera equipment and took it with me before I killed her.

Dr. Weber continued talking to me, but I was only halflistening, the night of Alison's murder still swimming around in my brain. I tried desperately to focus, to remember the exact moment that night when I had blacked out. I remembered I'd driven to the park, dumped the bag, and then—well, then I sat in my car and drank several sips of vodka from the bottle I'd kept hidden under my front seat. I wasn't drunk. I knew that. Perhaps three, maybe four sips, just enough to calm my nerves. I'd started to drive . . . yes, I remembered . . . that was when another migraine came on. I'd driven to a parking lot near the playground by our house, and then—the next thing I could remember was going home. That must have been when I blacked out. I don't remember leaving the parking lot, though, just pulling up in front of my house. I tried desperately to remember the time between, but it was gone. Missing.

"He thinks I killed her," I blurted out.

Dr. Weber looked at me with a puzzled expression. "Who thinks you killed who, dear?"

"If I killed her, wouldn't I remember it?" I asked, but what the doctor didn't realize was I hadn't been asking her. I was asking myself.

"I mean, could I have done what he says I did? It was him. I thought it was him, but—no, he was never that good of a liar. He thought he was . . ." As I stammered on, I could see the doctor's lips as she continued to talk to me, but I needed to figure this out. She wasn't a part of this puzzle. "If it wasn't him, though, it had to be someone else, but who would have even known Nathan was having an affair?"

The question hung in front of me for a few moments. "I knew he was having an affair!" I shouted the statement. "I know it sounds crazy. I planned to kill her, I did. When I saw she was pregnant, I knew he would never abandon his kid. Not after the way his dad had treated him, but I couldn't do it, I swear!"

"Ms. Foster, can you hear me?" Dr. Weber was shouting by that point, but I continued to ignore her.

My arms flailed, like windsocks in a storm, disconnected from my body as I attempted to push the doctor looming over me away. The guard was there now, trying to catch my free-flowing limbs. The doctor disappeared briefly before she reappeared with a syringe, but I was too busy solving this case to give a shit about her or her needle.

"He said it. He said he couldn't believe what I took from him." I was talking faster. "But I didn't, I can't remember—but I know I wouldn't have—" I realized the guard must have pinned my arms to my side when I tried to bang on my head with my palm but couldn't move my hands.

"She told him she was pregnant. He was so happy. I can remember that. Why can't I remember driving home? I tossed the bag. Didn't I? It wasn't bloody. There was no blood. I don't remember any blood."

"Elizabeth," Dr. Weber's voice briefly cut through my rantings before she was once again reduced to mutterings.

"I didn't have any other options. He was going to leave me. But I changed my mind. I know I did. I remember changing my mind. I didn't do it!" I felt the needle jab my arm, but I didn't care. I was going to figure out who the hell killed Alison.

"Duct tape, plastic, rope, a hunting knife." I named off the inventory list inside the bag I'd brought to Alison's home.

I closed my eyes tight as I tried to remember what I was missing from that night. I was there, ready to reclaim my husband, I saw the ultrasound, and I left. I was going to wait in the darkness with my hunting knife for her to return, and when she was asleep, I would use chloroform. That would make it easier when I pushed the blade into her heart. Then I would dismember her body with the reciprocating saw I'd brought and wrap her in plastic to dispose of it. I was sure I would remember the blood if I cut someone up.

"Fuck." I moaned, but it sounded odd. It was slow and quiet and not how I had intended it.

The chloroform. The prosecutor had figured out that I'd gone to the library and placed an order for it online and had it delivered to a PO Box. I'd set it up under a fake name forty-five minutes away from where I lived. I remembered the jury's gasps when the prosecutor showed the security footage from the post office of me picking up the package from the PO Box. I never denied I bought it, though. Of course, I bought it. I had to. I needed to get my husband back, but I changed my mind. Buying it and using it are two different things, I'd told Larry as we prepped for the trial. Nathan sat silent, watching from across the room.

Someone else killed Alison, didn't they? I felt my eyelids growing heavier. I blinked, and each time I did, the darkness before I reopened them lengthened.

"Elizabeth, don't fight it." The doctor's voice had overpowered my thoughts.

I didn't . . . kill . . . her . . . I thought. My mind was hazy. *Did I?*

∽

27

I watched the bartender as she spoke flirtatiously to the men across from her in their high-priced suits. She whipped her chestnut-brown hair to expose her golden-skinned shoulder, then tossed her head back in an exaggerated laugh in response to something one of the men had said. I recognized that laugh. It was one that men loved when they heard. It wasn't necessarily sincere, but it was effective.

The man who had shared the delightful statement picked up his drink and slid her a folded-up twenty with a wink. She dropped it into her tip pitcher and leaned forward to squeal a thank you. Her tactic had worked. A pretty girl had stroked the man's ego, and for her efforts, she was rewarded with a large tip.

As I sat there, I wondered if Alison had so easily swayed Nathan. I shifted my legs and crossed them in the opposite direction, playing with the wedge of lime on the edge of my glass as I pondered the question. Nathan told me how he'd always loved having the prettiest girl in the room on his arm.

Was I no longer the prettiest girl to him? Had he upgraded to someone he felt was worthier of his affection?

I shook my head in hopes of shaking loose the doubts that had started to take hold in my mind. When I did, my attention was drawn to the woman behind the bartender—the woman in the mirror. I didn't recognize her, and it frightened me. Her eyes had dark circles under them, and her blond hair was pulled up into a messy ponytail. There was no risk of any of the men in that bar seeking attention from her. From me. I was certainly no longer the most beautiful woman in the room. I was shocked and angered as I stared at my reflection at what I'd allowed myself to turn into.

This needed to end. I couldn't keep watching Nathan living his life with that woman. I'd made excuses when I decided to sneak into her home . . . their home and hide the spy cams. As I drove several towns over to purchase the equipment, I explained to the clerk I was confident our cleaning woman was stealing from us. Jesus, I couldn't stand how I sounded. The woman who came to clean my house was one of the sweetest and most caring women I had ever met. At that moment, I'd felt overcome with guilt as I thought of the brownies she had brought after she discovered we'd lost the baby. The lie rolled so easily off my tongue, but I convinced myself it was for a good cause. I needed the shopkeeper to assume I was another suburban woman with too much time and entitlement on her hands.

When I waited in the shadows to make sure Alison had left for work before breaking into her home to hide the cameras, I told myself it was for Nathan. Just as the bartender had flipped her hair and laughed at the man's likely humorless joke, Alison had found Nathan's weakness. If I could see inside, hear what they said to one another, I could figure out how to break the spell she used to capture my husband. The cameras would help me fill in the gaps and understand how she'd managed to weasel her way into his life—our lives.

Nathan wasn't innocent. I'd known that. But I also knew he would never do this to me without a bit of coercing. Not after everything we had been through together. But since installing the cameras, all I had witnessed were longing glances between the two of them—playful flirting in the kitchen, like we used to do. Passionate lovemaking. I knew I shouldn't have watched, but I couldn't look away.

The woman who now looked back at me from the mirror behind the bartender spoke to me. She told me I'd gone too far. I'd lost too much of who I was. This needed to end. I couldn't continue the way I had, or not much of the woman I was would survive. If I had any hope of getting my life back, something had to change. I had to confront Nathan ... What would I say? What could I have said? What if he'd decided we were over, and he was waiting for me to come to that realization.

My eyes locked onto my reflection, and I saw the corners of my mouth twitch and an eyebrow lift. The formation of a smile began as the first seed of the plan started to hatch in my brain. I lifted the glass that held the vodka soda to my lips and took another sip.

Color returned to my cheeks as I allowed the plan to continue to form. There was a glimmer in my eyes, and I thought I could see who I used to be for a moment. Alison had known what she was doing. She knew full well when she seduced my husband he was a married man. As a result of that knowledge, she should also have been fully aware that her actions would have consequences. In a way, she'd chosen her destiny. It wasn't my doing at all.

Alison Adams would have to die. Maybe he loved us both, but I wasn't willing to share him. I would have to do this for him. I would have to remove the conflicting object of his affection. It was what was best for everyone.

∼

28

There could be no body. If there were a body, it would create an investigation. Perhaps Nathan would even be a suspect. After all, he owned the home she was living in, and he was having an affair with this woman. No, this would have to be a well-researched plan. It would need to look like Alison left that she chose to run away.

I started to research the woman who consumed Nathan's evenings. She was from a small town in the Midwest. Her mother had passed away when she was in high school, and soon after her graduation, her father remarried and started a second family. She had a half sister. She didn't talk with them a tremendous amount, so I wasn't too worried about them as a loose end.

She did, however, have a best friend who could pose a problem. As part of my surveillance of Alison, I discovered they met for lunch at least twice a week. They were close. I watched hours of footage of them speaking over the phone. She told her friend everything. Alison even used Nathan's name when she talked to the woman. That was enough for me to want to *smash her perfect button nose into her skull. She had no regard for Nathan's reputation and the damage that she could be doing to it.*

Powerful men were always susceptible to a scandal. If she loved Nathan as I did, she would have done anything to protect him. That alone was proof she could never be the better match for him. But the best friend still posed a problem. She was aware of the affair, and if Alison were going to disappear off the face of the earth, it would create suspicions.

My best friend, Emily, had been my roommate in college, my maid of honor, and despite moving to Florida for a job as a news anchor, we made sure to speak to each other over the phone at least once a week.

She would have questioned if I disappeared, and I had to assume Alison's friend would do the same. I would need to come up with a reason for her leaving that was so sound, so iron-clad, nobody would question it.

Disposing of the body, thanks to the internet, would be much easier. On my trusty corner machine in the back of the library, I discovered there are many ways to dispose of a body. One site I stumbled across suggested if one is in a hurry, the easiest way is to take a boat out to sea, weigh it down and drop the corpse into the deepest part of the ocean you can find. I was near the coast, and the idea of sea creatures disposing of the body for me was a tempting thought, but there were too many ways I could think of to get caught with the body.

In a fascinating twist, I also discovered many dark corners of the internet where people were interested in purchasing body parts. There were various reasons for this ranging from perversion to fascination, all the way to scientific experiments that weren't exactly above board. I also felt that option left far too many opportunities for me to end up in prison.

For a long time, I considered drugging Alison and then setting fire to her home while she slept, but ultimately, it left too much up to chance that she would survive. If Alison had narrowly escaped death, it would undoubtedly send Nathan into a spiral where he questioned what life would look like without her. I didn't need him confusing his feelings for actually being in love with her.

I was intrigued by the notion of feeding her body to pigs. Still, I ultimately decided that dissolving her body made the most sense without easy access to any livestock. It wasn't a fast process, so it obviously could not be done at her home. Instead, I'd rent a storage facility and secure several industrial barrels along with the chemicals I would need to turn pretty little Alison into a gelatinous consistency. I would then dispose of those remains over time throughout various storm drains in the city.

It would take a solid stomach and a lot of determination, but I'd known this was the moment that would determine how hard I was willing to fight for my marriage.

The killing itself would have to happen quickly as I would need to get back home so as not to raise much suspicion from Nathan. The plan was perfect.

I'd need to carefully collect all the items using cash and purchase them from small shops far away from where I lived. I would use chloroform after she was asleep to ensure she would not awake during the process. She was wrong for seducing my husband, but that didn't mean she needed to suffer.

While she slept, I would plunge the hunting knife I had

acquired into her heart. After I'd determined she was no longer breathing, I would start the dismemberment using a saw. I only needed to make the pieces small enough for me to carry. I would wrap them in plastic and blankets and towels before placing them into bags to reduce the risk of blood in my vehicle.

I would need to dispose of Alison's car at the train station. I also would need to purchase a train ticket using her credit card. If I were going to get away with all of this, I needed to execute the plan flawlessly. Anything less would result in prison. Worse, if Nathan ever found out what I had done, he would never forgive me.

∼

29

I used to pick apart fairy-tale cartoons as a child. A beautiful young girl, so happy and content with the world that she would sing cheerful songs as birds flew around her. It wasn't the mice turning into horses or a frog turning into a prince that I couldn't seem to wrap my head around. No, it was the sheer joy these girls felt being alive. I'd always known the world was a vicious place, so it didn't surprise me when I found out it was kicking me in my teeth.

Planning Alison's murder had given me something to focus on during the recent months. The affair had helped me see just how much of a fairy tale I had been living in before Alison. Yes, we'd struggled to have a child, but now I realized if we could overcome this, we would be able to triumph over anything.

Once Alison was gone from our lives, Nathan would lean back into our marriage. I would be a more involved wife. I would take an active role in the things he loved. I would make an effort with his co-worker's wives.

Things had already started to change. I was eating well again and exercising. I'd even started going back to my *favorite gym. Nathan noticed too. He had started to desire me like he used to. If things kept going like they were, there was a chance I wouldn't even have to go through with the plan. There was a chance Nathan would leave Alison on his own. I didn't want to kill the poor girl. It would have been a far more desirable outcome if he ended things.*

I'd even fallen behind on reviewing the tapes from Alison's house. It no longer consumed my thoughts. Nathan had given me a deep and passionate kiss, groping my breast before he left for work. It was like Alison didn't exist anymore. It made me wonder whether he had ended things with her. Had I missed it because I had gotten behind on the tapes? Did I not need to worry anymore because the problem took care of itself while finding myself and my marriage again? I thought perhaps I should be thanking Alison for helping us rekindle that magic.

I glanced at my watch and decided to go to the afternoon cycling class instead. I pulled on the latch that lowered the steps to the attic and climbed up into the bean bag chair I had placed up there. I flipped open the laptop I purchased with cash and downloaded the videos I had not yet seen from the cloud. I ticked up the speed of the video and watched the scenes unfold at high speed.

A lot of the time, Alison was alone, which didn't surprise me. I noticed Nathan had been home more as of late. It felt like we had reversed roles lately. She answered the phone, and I slowed the video to listen. Based on the conversation that unfolded, I assumed it was her best friend. She was complaining that Nathan never seemed to have time for her anymore, and my heart fluttered. At one point, I saw her run off the frame and heard vomiting noises in the toilet. I am not proud to say that I took a little satisfaction in seeing that she was sick. She was always put together and perfect, so it felt satisfying that she was susceptible to the same illnesses as the rest of us mere mortals.

I ticked up the speed of the video again until I caught a glimpse of what looked like her and Nathan arguing. I paused and returned the tape to the standard rate of speed.

"What is going on with you?" she asked.

"I told you, nothing." My eyes darted to the time of the video. It had only happened yesterday. I was elated to see I was correct, and there was a rift growing between them. I continued watching with hopeful eyes.

"It's like you'd rather be with her than with me."

I smiled at her statement. He was falling back in love with me. She could see it too.

"You're ridiculous," he stated, not denying her accusation.

"You said you wanted to marry me." She started to weep. I recognized that tactic immediately. It was the hair toss or fake exuberant laughter, the fluttering of eyelashes, or the pouty lips. All were things I'd seen Alison use to manipulate my husband.

"Don't fall for it, babe!" I shouted at the screen.

"I do!" he exclaimed before he shook his head. "I mean, I did."

It felt like my heart was going to burst out of my chest at that moment. Nathan corrected himself. He no longer wanted to marry her. She was losing him. Perhaps, she had already lost him.

Her crocodile tears stopped immediately, and her jaw fell as she looked at him in disbelief. "What?"

"I mean—I want to marry you, but I'm already married."

"You said you were going to get a divorce," she reminded him.

"I didn't exactly say that," he protested. *"I said I didn't think Lizzy could handle a divorce right now."*

"Oh fuck you!" she shouted. *"You know what you were saying."*

Nathan started to rub his forehead. He would do this when he wanted to yell but was trying not to.

"Go ahead," I squealed. *"Let the bitch have it."*

"I pay for this very nice house that you live in, Alison. I made sure you weren't part of the layoffs at the office. And thanks to me, you have a very comfortable lifestyle." As he explained the things he provided her with, I felt nauseous. I hated that he took the money he worked for and gave it to her.

"So I'm just some kind of whore to you?" she snapped as she turned the waterworks back on.

"That's not fair, and you know it. I never lied to you about the feelings I had for my wife."

"She doesn't love you back," Alison hissed.

"Maybe not." I felt my eyes grow wet when I realized how Nathan thought I felt about him. I felt guilty that I had ever let our relationship get to the point where he doubted my feelings for him. *"But I care about her, and after everything we've been through, I can't just leave her. Not after the baby."*

I wished I could reach through that screen and throw my arms around my husband's neck, that I could tell him I still loved him. Tell him we could come back from this and have the family we had always dreamed of. Maybe this time, it would be adoption or a surrogate. No matter what it took, I would be by his side, and I would never let us reach this point again.

"What about our baby?" Alison asked. I stopped the video

as if by instinct and rewound it for ten seconds. "What about our baby?" I did it again . . . and again. "Our baby."

Alison disappeared off-screen for a moment, bringing back what appeared to be a photograph. Nathan took it from her hands. He stood there, looking at it, speechless until, at last, I heard him say, "Are you serious?"

She nodded, and his face lit up.

"You're going to be a dad." When I heard her say the statement, I slammed the lid of the laptop shut. My head started to spin. He wasn't leaving her. He never would. Not if she was having his child. His dad had not been part of his life, and he'd always told me he was never going to be that kind of dad. I was going to lose him forever.

Red filled my vision. The plan was back on.

∽

30

I awoke, shook by the nightmare I'd emerged from. I attempted to pull the blankets over my head to create a cocoon, but I quickly realized my arms were strapped at my sides. My head snapped upward, and I found my entire body was strapped to a hospital bed.

I wiggled to see if perhaps I could get loose, but it was in vain. In quiet desperation, I looked around the room, and near the door, I saw a familiar woman in a lab coat.

The room started to shift around me. I recalled the nightmare I had just awoken from. It wasn't just a nightmare, though. It had been my memories. I was going to kill Alison.

I saw the ultrasound, and I decided not to kill her. Hadn't I? I wasn't sure anymore. I wasn't sure of anything. Nathan hadn't killed Alison. I saw that in his eyes. Was he a better liar than I had realized? No, it was apparent after all this time he was still in so much pain. He lost another chance at fatherhood. My heart started to race as the question went through my mind, could I have? Could I have ended Nathan's chance at fatherhood by killing that woman?

"You're awake." The doctor's voice cut through my thoughts. "That was quite the episode you had."

"Episode?"

"You don't remember?" Dr. Weber asked, and I shook my head.

"I had to give you something to sedate you," she explained.

"Doctor," I started, the nightmare still filling my thoughts. "What can someone do when they black out?" I couldn't stop wondering why I couldn't remember driving home? What happened during that time?

"What do you mean?" Dr. Weber studied my face.

"I mean, can you still do things?"

"What kind of things?" the doctor probed, shaking her head in confusion.

I hesitated. I couldn't come out and ask if it were possible that I brutally murdered someone during a blackout. "Like, could you still drive a car?"

She considered my question for a moment. "If you black out to the point of unconsciousness, of course not." I sighed a breath of relief, but then the doctor pulled the feeling away just as quickly. "But then there are some people, especially those who might be processing a traumatic event in their lives, where it's not so much as passing out as losing time."

"What do you mean lose time?" I asked, trying not to sound as desperate as I felt.

"Well, they can continue to function completely normal, but they would have absolutely no recollection of what happened during the time. Think of it as a mechanism for the mind to protect itself when an event is too hard for a person to deal with. Is this something you are worried about, my dear?"

"No, just curious, I guess." I forced a smile.

"You were out for quite a while," she added as she moved in to wrap the blood pressure cuff around my arm. "You know we can prescribe you something to help you with those nightmares if they're interfering with your sleep."

"Nightmares?" I asked, a confused line stitched across the middle of my brow.

She nodded as she undid the cuff and started to unstrap me. "We had to strap you to the bed at one point because you had started tossing so violently."

"I was?"

"Yes, you kept muttering. I'm sorry, I didn't mean to."

I forced a laugh. "Huh, that strange."

"I think it's probably a good idea for you to have some extra sessions with Dr. Clarkson," she added.

I smiled at the woman. "I'm fine. I get anemic sometimes. I'm sure that's it." Dr. Clarkson was the prison psychiatrist. He loved prescribing meds to the women in here to make them more what he called compliant to their surroundings, which meant zombie-like.

She flipped a page over on the chart in front of her. "Actually, we did have some blood work done, and . . ." She paused as she read through the words. "Your tox screen was clean." I tried my best not to take offense to the surprise in her voice. "And huh, you are slightly anemic. I'm going to prescribe some iron pills for you."

Iron pills were not going to cure what was plaguing me. I needed to figure out who killed my husband's mistress, even if that person was me.

"We should probably have a CT scan done as well," Dr. Weber noted as she jotted something down onto my chart.

I wiggled my wrists in the restraints that were digging into my flesh. "CT scan?"

"If you've had migraines in the past, it could be a symptom of something else. We just want to make sure everything's good," she replied.

Everything wasn't good, though. I'd realized there was a chance I was in precisely the place I should have been.

31

I hadn't had a visitor or a letter in two weeks. Temporary restrictions were placed on me, pending a psychological evaluation. Luckily, all it took to fool Dr. Clarkson was a big smile, long eyelashes, and a ridiculous excuse about how sometimes you just got a little crazy when it was your time of the month.

Amazingly he was what passed for psychological health care in this place. He was terrible, and the fact that he was offering that sort of care at a women's prison should have been criminal in itself.

Any psychiatrist of any account would have recognized Savannah's depression during her intake interview. Dr. Clarkson spent two minutes with her and stamped her with a clean bill of mental health.

I passed my review, though, and after the two-week hold, I would soon receive any mail that had been held back, and now the first visiting day since my lockdown had finally come. At that point, I don't think I would have cared who came to see me. I probably even would have welcomed another scolding from Brook. What awaited me on that first day out of lockdown was so much better than my sister, though.

"Foster, your lawyer, is here to see you," the guard, Red, barked at me from the entrance of my cell.

∽

My lawyer sat across from me and flipped through her notes. I hadn't seen or heard from her in months, the only interaction with her office being when the paralegal refused to do a wellness check on Evelyn.

"I'm sorry I haven't been in sooner." She started. "The prosecutor's office took their sweet time getting us the case files. They tried to tell us we had to get them from your previous lawyer like I was some kind of idiot. Sometimes these guys are such pricks, you know?"

I liked Lauren. She never pulled any punches, and I always understood right where my case stood, unlike Larry, who always told me everything was going to be okay and I needed to quit worrying so much.

"It's fine," I said, even though I had been going out of mind waiting for word from her on how the appeal was coming along. A part of me hadn't wanted to know, though, since, in Lauren's first visit, she had warned that with the way things stood, it didn't look good.

I noticed her fingernails weren't painted. That was one of the things I missed about the outside. Well, one of the very long lists of things. Manicures. What I had considered as essential self-care was a luxury inside this place. I pushed the doubts in my mind away and told myself if I ever got out of this place, I would enjoy the little things—a mani/pedi, a blowout, an afternoon facial.

I braced myself as I waited for her to break the news that my appeal probably didn't have a snowball's chance in hell in going anywhere. She settled on a page in her notebook and looked up at me. One of my knees started to bounce under the table as I waited anxiously.

"I've heard you've been having some trouble in here," she stated, returning her gaze to the papers in front of her. I wondered how much she knew. I'd been under medical supervision, and I knew they could only disclose so much.

I forced a tight-lipped smile before I replied dismissively. "It was nothing, just an overreaction to me being a little anemic." I'd decided there was no need for Lauren to know the utter chaos that had broken out inside my head. Her job was to focus on getting me out of here, and I didn't want to say anything that might distract her from her objective. I just hoped I didn't figure out that her job was hopeless because they, in fact, already had the right person behind bars.

She licked her lips. "So you know how your last attorney went with the defense that there was a random intruder in the house that came after you left that night?"

I nodded. "Yeah, that didn't play out very well for me, though, did it?"

"Well, get this. While one of our assistants was going through the boxes of evidence the prosecutor sent over, they noticed a side note about the knife."

I shook my head. "They had video of me purchasing

it, so if you're going to say it wasn't mine, that won't work."

She lifted a hand. "No, that's not it all. There was supposed to be a report attached that broke down all substances found on the knife, but that report was never sent over," she explained.

"I don't understand what any of that means."

"It means that a key piece of evidence was withheld at your trial."

"What does that mean?" I attempted to clarify again.

"Based on that, your appeal is probably going to get you another trial," she said.

"Another trial?"

"Yup, we confirmed with your previous lawyer the document had never been sent over," she continued.

"I don't understand. Why would that matter?"

She flashed me a grin before she explained. "Because when I finally was able to obtain a copy of that report, it said there was an unknown source of DNA on that knife."

"What?" I gasped in disbelief. Could it be that I was right, and there was no way I would have actually killed Alison?

She nodded and leaned back against the chair as she explained. "The police had samples from anyone who had been in that house, and it wasn't a match. It also didn't match anyone in the state database. Our office has put in a request for the sample to be run through the federal DNA database."

"Okay, you're losing me again," I said, my eyes fixed intensely on her.

"No matter what the DNA results are, this is information the jury didn't have. Another DNA source on the murder weapon could have created reasonable doubt, so I feel confident we'll be able to get you a new trial."

"I'm getting out of here?" I practically leaped out of my skin as I said the words.

"Slow down." She raised a hand cautiously. "That paperwork has already been submitted, but it does take a while. In the meantime, if we can figure out who the DNA belongs to, maybe we can piece together an ironclad defense." I fought the urge to leap across the table and throw my arms around Lauren's neck.

"I can't believe this is happening."

She smiled. "Hang in there, okay? We're doing everything we can to get you out of this place."

"Wait a second," I said as the excitement of the initial news dissipated. "It wasn't Nathan's DNA?"

She looked back at her notes and flipped through a couple of pages before she replied. "It looks like he voluntarily gave a sample, so I would say it wasn't a match."

Had I been that wrong? As soon as I saw how he was looking at me, I realized that perhaps I had been blaming the wrong person all along. If it wasn't me, and it wasn't Nathan, though, I couldn't imagine who it could have been.

"Why wouldn't the police have followed up on the DNA they found on the knife?" I ground my teeth after I asked the question, furious the information hadn't come out at my trial.

She shook her head. "I can't be sure, but my guess is when they discovered the evidence against you, it was the path of least resistance."

Path of least resistance. I broke down the statement in my head. Had I lost the last year of my life because it was the most straightforward explanation of what had happened that night?

"Now, I don't want you to get your hopes up too much that this will get resolved quickly."

"Are you kidding me? This is the best news I've gotten since I was arrested," I replied.

She smiled. "As long as you know that the courts tend to move at their own pace."

Lauren started to gather up her notes.

"Wait. Before you go," I chimed, then explained the situation about Savannah. Maybe, if we were lucky, we would both figure a way out of our current circumstances. Lauren said she would look into it and see if she could do anything to help her.

∼

32

My toes curled, and I stiffened as I stared at the bunk above me. Wedged into the slats were quotes from some of my favorite books, but even they couldn't seem to quiet my mind. I'd always thought Nathan was manipulative when he said the things that made me appear to be delusional, but it hadn't been because he was plotting against me. He had been as wrong about me as I had been about him.

It felt like discovering that Nathan nor myself had killed Alison should have made me overcome with joy, but all it did was create more questions. Who could have possibly known what was happening in our lives? Who would have known about the affair in the first place? Perhaps it had been someone at Nathan's work. They had left together for lunches, so they hadn't exactly been inconspicuous.

It didn't make sense, though. If that were the case, how did the person know about me and what I had been up to? How did they know I would have gone to her house that night? If they were following me and discovered what I had tossed into that park trash that night, was it just a crime of opportunity for them? No, something so violent and savage felt personal.

Alison's best friend, the one she was always talking to on the phone. She knew about Nathan. Was there more to this faceless woman? I'd only ever heard one side of the conversations, but it never seemed like it was more than friendly gossiping from Alison's responses.

"Hey, you're going to miss visitation if you don't get over there," Ruby warned, tapping my shoulder as she walked past my bunk.

"Huh?" I moaned, snapping back to reality. "Oh, right," I added as I stood and shuffled into the hall. I knew after our last visits I would never see Nathan or Evelyn again, and since no approval request was sent to me, my visitor that day had to be someone on my approved list. I assumed it was most likely my mother. It was about that time, and after discovering I had been put on visitor restrictions for two weeks, I'm sure she was chomping at the bit to figure out what I'd done wrong now.

I glanced out a window as I moved down the long hall toward the visitors' room. The barbed wire felt strangely comforting for the first time. When I'd thought Nathan was the killer, it had at least given me a sense of who the enemy was. With the new information coming to light that an unknown source of DNA was found on the murder weapon, the world felt much scarier. On the other side of that barbed wire, someone out there hated Nathan and me so much that they wanted to destroy our lives. Until I'd managed to figure it out, I somehow felt safer inside, surrounded by these women.

I started to shake, and tears rushed down my cheeks when I caught sight of Emily in the visitors' room. She was smiling at me and waving enthusiastically. I hurried across the room. At that moment, I wasn't sure if any other face in the world would have made me feel better. We embraced briefly, though I'd wished it could have been longer.

"I can't believe you're here!" I exclaimed. It wasn't easy for Emily to come from where she lived in Florida. As a single mom and not knowing many people where she lived, she had to bring her son with her when she traveled.

"Are you kidding? As soon as your mom told me what a hard time you were having, there was no way I wasn't going to hop on the first plane."

"Where's Tyler?" I asked, imagining the sweet boy sitting in the waiting room with a guard for his mother to return.

"Well . . ." She grinned as she drew out the word. "There's been a development." She waved her finger in front of me, flaunting a large diamond on it.

"Are you fucking kidding me?" I squealed, excitement exploding from me. One of the guards flashed me a warning by lifting a finger, and I nodded apologetically. "Are you fucking kidding me?" I asked again, but this time in a whisper.

She smiled as she stared at the ring. "Roger said he wants to adopt Tyler too. He's back in Florida with him right now. It's so cute seeing them together. Tyler gets so excited every time he sees him."

"Oh, Em, I am so happy for you," I said, a smile etched across my face. Tyler's actual father had been from a brief affair at Emily's previous job, and he'd made it clear he wanted nothing to do with raising him. Despite Emily acting like it hadn't bothered her, I knew she was heartbroken, and that was a big reason she took the anchor job in Florida.

She lifted her brows. "I hope it doesn't seem like I'm bragging."

"What? No, of course not. You're my best friend."

"I know, with you in here and all, I just didn't know how to tell you."

"Well, any chance you have room for your best friend in your wedding party?" I asked.

She shook her head in confusion. "What?"

"My lawyer says there's a real shot at me getting another trial."

"Oh my God, are you serious?" She gasped. "That's amazing. Your mom didn't say anything."

"Yeah, well, I haven't told her yet."

Emily tilted her head. "I know she can be the queen bitch, but she still worries about you."

I waved my hands at her in defense. "I know, I know, and I do plan to tell her. It just all happened so fast."

Emily's face was glowing, and all I could think about was how much I'd missed having her in my life. So many times, I had considered picking up the phone and telling her about Alison and Nathan's affair, but I knew she would have told me to leave him. "I don't understand. What exactly happened?"

"Apparently, they've found someone else's DNA at the crime scene," I started. "And that information was never disclosed to my attorney the first time around."

"No way, are you shitting me?" Emily's mouth dropped open in disbelief.

"Nope, hand to God," I swore as I lifted a single hand.

"So whose was it?" Her eyelashes fluttered, and I could see her chest stop moving as she held her breath, waiting for the information I had.

I shook my head. "They're running it through some federal database."

Her lips pressed together, and her brows lifted before she said. "Liz, that's amazing."

I nodded but then fell silent.

"So I don't get it then. This is amazing news. If your mom doesn't know, why would she have called me in such a tizzy?" she asked, not taking her eyes off my face.

I laughed as I considered all the many things that usually resulted in my mother being in a tizzy. "Oh, if I had to guess, it was probably the psych hold I got put on for two weeks."

Emily's eyes widened, and a concerned expression planted itself firmly on her alabaster skin. "What? Did something happen?"

I nodded and rolled my eyes as I started to explain. "I don't know. I guess it was seeing Nathan."

She stiffened, and a confused expression washed away the concern. "Wait, back up." She pulled her hands back and crossed her arms over her chest. "Nathan was here?"

I sighed. "Okay, so a lot has happened since I've last written you."

"I'd say so."

I proceeded to explain everything from the first visit from Dr. Evelyn Powell up until the moment I walked out and saw Emily's face smiling back at me.

"Oh my God, this is crazy. What are you going to do?" Emily asked.

I furrowed my brow. "What do you mean, what am I going to do?"

"You have to call your lawyers," she insisted.

I laughed. "For what?"

Emily shook her head and waved her hands wildly for a moment. "I don't know. None of that sounds normal, Liz. What kind of woman shows up here, trying to get you to sign divorce papers so she can marry your husband? She sounds unstable."

"It's not like that," I assured her. "She seems very nice. I think in another life, you and I would have actually been friends with her."

"Oh my God, you always do this," Emily huffed.

"Do what?" I asked defensively.

"See the best in people. This is exactly why you kept making excuses for Nathan."

"That's not fair. You know what he had been through." I always felt the need to defend Nathan from Emily's attacks for some reason. He was no longer my responsibility to protect, yet I still had trouble letting the habit die.

"Less than what you went through?" Her cheeks flushed red with frustration. "You carried that child inside you and then had to say goodbye to him. Did you go out and find the first man who would look your way to have an affair with?"

"I'm sure that's not how it happened," I said.

"Do you hear yourself? You're still defending him!"

"I am not," I protested even though she was right. "It's just . . ." I stopped myself, afraid that if I said the next words, the friend who had always believed in me would suddenly start looking at me differently.

"Just what?" she asked.

I shook my head. "Nothing." I wanted the smiling Emily back. The one who had just gotten engaged and was there to make me feel better.

"It's just what?" She was firm when she repeated herself, but I continued to resist. "I'm not going to let it drop until you tell me."

My shoulders slumped in defeat, and I leaned forward as I proceeded to whisper. "I don't remember everything from that night."

"What night?"

"The night Alison died," I replied.

"What do you mean when you say you don't remember everything?" she asked, her eyes fixed on my mouth.

I'm suddenly uncomfortable with her gaze and look away, worried that when I said the next words, Emily may look at me like Nathan had. Like I was a murderer. "There are parts of the night she died that I can't remember."

"Like what?" Emily pressed.

"Like I don't remember driving home after tossing the bag," I whispered.

Emily rolled her eyes. "So what? I don't remember much about my ride from the airport, but I know I'm here, so it must have happened."

"But what if they're right?"

"They're who?"

"Everyone." I let out a strangled breath before I managed to continue. "The jury, Nathan . . . what if I did kill her?"

Emily started laughing. "Don't be ridiculous. You remember leaving before she ever got home that night. That seems like the important part."

"Yeah, but what if I went back?" I started to reveal my doubts. "What if I'm blocking it out because it was so traumatic or something? What if I went back that night and killed her? Jesus, Em, I planned her murder. I bought all the supplies. Who does that?"

"Oh, for fuck's sake, Liz, I wanted to murder Nathan when I found out what he'd put you through, but I didn't, and that's because I am no more a killer than you are."

"I had every detail planned."

"I know. I was at the trial, and I heard all of it. And I still have zero doubt that you didn't kill that woman."

"I even planned out how I was going to get rid of the body. That doesn't sound like something a rational person does."

She tossed a hand into the air. "See, even more proof it wasn't you."

"What?"

"If you had planned to get rid of the body, why didn't you?"

I frowned. "I don't know."

"Don't you dare let that prick of a husband of yours convince you that you would ever be capable of doing it. That asshole! I could go strangle him right now with my bare hands." She huffed. "So you put more dedication into your fantasizing than other people do. It doesn't make you a killer. Do you know how many times I've fantasized about killing my co-anchor? I swear to God if he grabs my ass one more time, I may actually do it."

"I thought you were as capable of murder as I was."

"Okay, I wouldn't kill him, but that's my point. People say it and even think about it, but ending someone's life isn't as easy as you think. With every fiber of my being, I know you didn't kill Alison because you're not a killer. You left because that's who you really are."

"I don't know." I sighed and looked down at my hands sitting on the table in front of me. Were they capable of brutally murdering the woman who Nathan had been having an affair with? "Maybe."

"There's no maybe. You didn't do it. Period. We just have to figure out who did. Is there any chance the DNA they found belongs to someone Nathan hired?"

I shook my head as I recalled the look in Nathan's eyes when he had come to visit me. "I swear, this is not me defending him because up until a couple of weeks ago, I was convinced he did it, but I'm not so sure Nathan had anything to do with it anymore."

"Yeah, well . . ." Emily waved a hand in my direction dismissively. "Sorry if I don't jump on the 'Nathan is

Innocent' wagon. You've always had a blind spot when it comes to that man."

"Wait, hear me out," I begged. "He wanted to be a father more than anything."

"And you wanted to be a mother. What's your point?"

"I'm just saying I don't think he would have ever done anything to Alison if it would have hurt his child. At first, I thought maybe it was some twisted fucked-up thing his dad had done to his head in his childhood. Maybe he killed Alison because he didn't want a repeat of his life, but if you saw his face when he was here, Emily. He is convinced I killed her."

"Then what happened that night?"

I closed my eyes. "I remember leaving. I remember tossing the bag and cameras into the trash at the park. I didn't imagine it. Whoever killed Alison had to have been following me."

"Who would have even known you were watching her?"

I considered her question silently.

"I wish I knew."

"Wait," Emily started, and it looked as if a light bulb were going off in her head. "Nathan's dad is some crazy rich dude, right?"

"I already thought of that," I replied. "He's barely been involved with Nathan's life besides giving him some money here and there. Honestly, I don't think he cares enough to give a shit if Nathan got some office bimbo pregnant."

"No, hear me out," Emily continued. "Isn't it like some big secret who his dad is?"

"I mean, yeah, I guess," I answered. "I think some people have their suspicions, but nobody would ever say anything."

"Do you think there's a chance Alison knew who his dad was?" Emily asked.

I considered her question. "I doubt Nathan would have told her, but it doesn't mean she didn't figure it out. I'm sure people talk around his office. He was always bitching about how people were insinuating he didn't earn his job title."

"Right," Emily gasped. "So what if Alison got greedy?"

I shook my head. "What do you mean?"

"What if she threatened to reveal to the world that he was the grandfather of her baby?"

"Why do that?"

"Why do you think she set her sights on Nathan in the first place? Maybe she thought he was never going to leave you, so she decided to try to get a payday another way."

"Are you saying Nathan's elderly father brutally murdered Alison?" I asked, my voice laced with skepticism.

"Well, not himself." She started. "But he very well may have hired someone to follow her, and then when he saw you there at the house, maybe he followed you to the park and saw what you dumped in the trash. What if he called Nathan's old man to report back and Daddy dearest saw an opportunity to clean up the problem."

"You really think he would have done something that could have possibly implicated his son in the murder?"

"Maybe that's where the tip came from. When they

started looking at Nathan for the murder, he decided it was time to toss you to the wolves." I collapsed onto the table with a huff after Emily finished laying out her walk-through of the crime.

"Jesus, I mean it's out there, but not impossible," I replied.

"Damn straight!" Emily exclaimed.

"My lawyer says they are waiting to see if they can have the DNA run through the federal database."

"Maybe I should reach out to your lawyer with this theory," Emily suggested.

Instinctively, I reached across the table and placed my fingertips on top of hers. "Let's wait for now. If there's a chance he is behind all of this, I don't want to think what he would do to you if he caught wind of what you were saying."

"I'm not scared of that old man," she stated defiantly.

"I know you're not." I smiled. "I'm just saying it's all conjecture at this point. Let's just wait until we know more, okay?"

She pursed her lips. "Okay. For now."

I nodded and thanked her. "I'm so lucky to have you," I added. Sadness filled me as I knew it was almost time to say goodbye.

∽

33

I stepped into the infirmary with butterflies in my stomach. I was about to learn what the CT scan might have revealed. The most logical conclusion I'd come to was a brain tumor. I hated to admit it, but it made sense. I'd read a brain tumor could cause a person to behave in ways they would never have under normal circumstances. That described what had been happening to me perfectly. Planning to murder someone wasn't exactly normal behavior for me.

"Hello," I said after I cleared my throat to get the doctor's attention.

"Elizabeth!" the woman exclaimed as she turned to greet me. She guided me to have a seat on the table, and I felt like I might keel over from the anticipation. "How are you doing today?"

"I'll be doing better if you tell me I don't have a brain tumor."

The woman repeatedly blinked with a confused look

before she started to laugh. "A brain tumor? Heavens no, what would give you an idea like that?"

"You ordered a CT scan," I replied plainly.

"Lots of people have CT scans. It doesn't mean the only thing it could be is a brain tumor." She smiled at me before she added, "And yours came back completely normal."

"What? How does that make sense? Something is clearly wrong with me."

The doctor hesitated.

"What is it?" I pressed.

"Liz, have you ever been scanned for postpartum depression?" The doctor looked at me with pity, and I found myself wishing I had something I could hide behind.

"No, I'm not a mom," I said dismissively.

"Oh." She blinked in confusion as she picked up my file and started to flip through the pages before she landed on the part she had been searching for. "Hmph, that's strange. Your medical records say you've given birth."

I nodded. "Well, I did, but he didn't make it."

"I'm so sorry." Her sympathy hung in the air, and I suddenly felt uncomfortable.

"Look, I didn't kill my baby, okay?"

She shook her head and smiled. "And nobody is saying you did. What I'm saying is even though your baby didn't survive, your body still went through the same thing as every other mother."

"I get headaches and black out because I'm sad?" I laughed after I posed the question.

"Postpartum isn't that simple. It's actually a pervasive problem, and it's believed eighty percent of mothers will experience it at some point in their lives. It usually goes away in a couple of weeks, but it can be a lingering and persistent issue in some rare cases. It wouldn't surprise me if you had PTSD from the loss of your child that was compounded by postpartum."

I shook my head as I processed the information being tossed at me. "But it's been so long. How am I still having headaches and stuff?"

"You've been shoved into a tough change in circumstance. Prison isn't easy on even the strongest of people."

I hesitated before I asked the question that had been weighing on my mind since Nathan's visit. "Is there any chance I could have killed someone and not remembered it?"

She stood quietly, and I could tell that she was surprised by my question. "Ms. Foster, I am not an expert by any means. That's a question for someone with—"

"Doc, I'm not asking you to testify in court or anything. I want to know your opinion. Could someone who is suffering from this have killed someone and not remember?"

She sighed before answering the question. "Perhaps. There's something called postpartum psychosis—"

"Psychosis? So I'm crazy?" I cried.

"That's not what I'm saying."

"So what are you saying?" I asked.

"I think we can get you help. There are medications we can try, and with therapy, I think we can help you get on the other side of this thing."

I thought about how I had planned Alison's murder and the way it felt as I had stood in her house and looked at that ultrasound. The moment I had realized the monster I had allowed myself to turn into. "Do you think you can help me?"

The doctor reached out and gripped my hand. "I think so."

I didn't have much faith in any therapy that Dr. Clarkson had to offer, but the diagnosis at least gave me some answers. I'd allowed my jealousy and rage to turn me into the kind of person who could have thought it was a rational decision to place cameras in a woman's home. A person who would purchase a knife with the intention of killing someone. With this diagnosis, I could at least start moving toward finding my way back to the person I was.

∼

34

The following weeks were filled with visits to the infirmary for blood work and adjustments to medications, as well as visits with Dr. Clarkson. Every visit was the same with him. He would ask me questions about my childhood and if I had ever been touched inappropriately. I made sure to make a mental note that I would file an official complaint about his incompetence if I ever got out of this place. I started to devour any reading I could get my hands on from the library about postpartum depression. It was like peering through a looking glass into my brain.

The reading kept me busy as I waited to hear from my lawyer about the news of the DNA database trace. As the fog in my mind had started to clear, I had begun to explore all kinds of theories about who could have killed Alison. There was still the harsh reality with my recent diagnosis it could have been me, but I'd begun to dive deeper into other ideas with Emily's recent visit. Perhaps it had been Nathan's father. But Alison also had a lot of unknowns. There were people in her life I knew nothing about. She had a stepmother and half sister. What were their relationships like? Or maybe my idea of her having an affair with another married man could have had some truth to it. Either way, Emily's idea that I could have been followed that night, presenting the killer with a crime of opportunity, was stuck in my brain. When Lauren finally got me out of this place, I was going to figure out who was behind this.

I'd had a visit from my mom last week, but besides that, it had been quiet. I'd been so deep in my research on postpartum I hadn't minded. Today, though, my name was on the call sheet for a visitor. Today, I would have to put my reading on hold briefly.

I stepped into the visitors' room, and my face went blank when I saw Evelyn Powell staring back at me. Her eyes were swollen, and I could tell she'd been crying. Her gaze was intense as I approached. *How long had it been since I'd seen her?* Six, seven weeks, maybe more? I recalled the letter I'd sent her. The letter where I put it all out there. The letter where I confessed to my part in the death of Alison.

I purchased the knife that killed her. I planned the murder. I provided everything the murderer needed. The murderer, the word stuck in my head. So much had changed since I'd written that letter. I understood what drove me to such irrational behavior. I was sick, but I was working on getting better.

I wasn't sure how I felt when I sat down across from Evelyn. A part of me was concerned for her, but I could see now what Emily had been trying to tell me. It wasn't healthy for me to be talking to this woman. It wasn't normal for her to come here and ask of me what she did.

"Are you okay?" I surprised myself with the words that came out of my mouth. In my head, I had thought of saying so many other things. I thought to tell her she couldn't come here anymore. I thought of telling her I didn't want to be part of what was going on between her and Nathan. I thought of telling her about my lawyer's discovery of the DNA and I didn't need her anymore. Somehow though, when I spoke, all I had was *are you okay?*

She offered a single nod of her head before stating in a steely voice, "I got your letter."

I thought of my letter again. The one where I poured out my heart and tried to convince her Nathan had killed Alison even though I was no longer convinced of it myself. I wished I had never sent it.

"I'm sorry," I offered. "I should have never sent that."

She pulled a stack of papers from her lap and placed them on the table. "If you need to read them over first, I understand. I included an addressed and stamped envelope."

I knew immediately what they were. "So you still want to marry him?"

She hesitated and avoided looking at me when she answered. "I love him."

"You've been crying," I stated, ignoring her declaration.

"I don't know what you're talking about."

"Your eyes are red and puffy."

"Allergies," she answered quickly.

"I see," I said, nodding.

"So you'll sign them?" she asked, and I thought she sounded desperate.

I considered her question. When I had written off Nathan as my husband, it was because I had assumed he was a killer and had framed me for murder. Now, though, things had changed with all the recent things that had come to light, including the DNA. But what about my marriage? It wasn't only that he had an affair. It had been so easy for both of us to assume the other one capable of such savagery. What did it say about our relationship? No. My marriage to Nathan was over no matter what happened or who killed Alison. I could see now that we were fundamentally broken.

"If that's what you want," I said at last.

She stiffened. "It is."

"You know, he came to see me," I added.

"Yes, I know!" she snapped defensively. "Nathan tells me everything."

"Did he tell you he had every opportunity to ask me to sign these papers when he was here, but he didn't?" I asked.

"What are you trying to say?" she hissed, her cheeks growing a brighter shade of red.

"Nothing, I guess." I huffed as I decided it wasn't worth it.

"No, obviously you have something to say, so say it."

I shook my head. I felt sorry for her. I was the one in prison, but I could see how desperate she was to prove that what they had was love. It had been obvious to me that Nathan didn't really love her. He felt beholden, and that was it. I wondered if I had looked just as sad and hopeless when trying to convince myself that he loved me and not Alison.

"You deserve to be with someone who loves you," I said at last.

"He does love me!" she exclaimed. "He just wants to move on with his life. Don't you think he deserves that?"

I took a deep breath and exhaled it slowly in an attempt to remain calm. While Evelyn was the one who had come here in the first place, I was the one who had invited her to return again and again. I reminded myself that I hadn't been selfless in my actions. I had wanted something from her. I wanted her to help me prove Nathan's guilt and, by extension, my innocence. I didn't need that from her anymore. I didn't think Nathan had killed Alison any longer. My lawyer was going to be the one to help me get out of this place.

I could see Evelyn as she gritted her teeth. Something in her life had changed because she was obviously distraught. Was Nathan angry she had come to see me? Had he told her what he told me? That he was marrying her because of what she had done to help him? Whatever it was, I told myself it was no longer my concern. I was determined to focus on my health so when I was finally freed from this place, I could start over.

I'd already been dreaming about what I would do once all of this was behind me. I would never have imagined myself living in Florida, but suddenly, the idea of being close to my godson sounded like the best life I could imagine. I'd majored in journalism, so perhaps, Emily could help me get a job at the station. Even if it was writing ad copy, it would be something that was mine. Nobody would ever be able to take that away from me.

"Evelyn, I don't care how Nathan feels about you. If you say he loves you, great. I hope the two of you are very happy together." She seemed surprised by my statement.

She shook he head and narrowed her eyes. "What game are you playing at?"

"No game," I replied. "I just figured out I don't care what Nathan does with his life."

"I thought he was some scary killer, and if I wasn't careful, I was going to be next." It almost felt as if she had been taunting me. She felt awkward, wrong to me. I couldn't tell if she had been that way all along, and I just had never noticed or if something had changed.

I smiled at her, pleased that not one part of me felt any animosity toward her about her relationship with Nathan. I exhaled and released the muscles in my back and extended my fingers outward like they had shown us in a meditation class I was taking on Tuesday evenings. I sat there, looking at her as she waited for me to speak, growing impatient with each passing second.

"You know he thinks you're crazy," she added, tired of waiting for me to respond.

I nodded. "From his perspective, I can see why." I'd thought Nathan was a murderer. My hands weren't clean in all this. Maybe I didn't love him anymore. After all, he had brought Alison into our lives in the first place, but the rage I'd once held for him was gone.

"What is with you?" she demanded.

"I just don't see the point in this anymore."

"The point is you said you would sign these papers," she barked.

"Fine, I'll sign them." I wanted it all to be over. I didn't want to think about Nathan, Alison, or Evelyn again.

"Are you serious?" she asked, and I could tell she wasn't sure I was telling the truth.

I nodded.

Evelyn slid the papers over to me. "Do you need to have your lawyer look over them?"

I shook my head. "I don't want anything from Nathan. I'm sure they're fine." In prison, I'd learned how little I actually needed to survive.

And just as I'd promised Evelyn I would on that first day I met her, I signed the divorce papers.

∼

35

The corners of Evelyn's mouth twisted upward into a smile as she peered at my signature on the papers. She scooped them up and clutched them to her chest as she let out a strangled laugh.

I turned toward her, not shielding the disgusted look on my face. "Can you try to contain your excitement, at least until you're no longer sitting right across from me?"

"I'm sorry, I've never been a very good sport," she hissed as her demeanor shifted into someone who was completely unrecognizable. A sour taste developed in my mouth as I watched her, puzzled by what I was seeing.

"Evelyn, what are you— ?"

"Oh, for fuck's sake, will you shut the hell up?" My jaw dropped when I heard the words from the woman's mouth. She stiffened and swung her hair as she tossed it over one shoulder. "I have had to listen to you and your constant whining for months now. You can't imagine how exhausting it's been."

I shook my head as I tried to make sense of what was

unfolding in front of me. Why was she still here? I had signed her papers.

"I mean, Jesus, when you started talking about your baby, and I had to sit there and try to validate your feelings, it was practically torture." I bit the inside of my jaw to stop myself from screaming. "I honestly do not understand how Nathan put up with your incessant whining."

I swallowed hard. "What are you saying?"

"It was so easy. You couldn't wait to spill your guts. I have to say, though, I think I gave the performance of a lifetime. I mean sitting here and pretending I cared about all your little revelations when I already knew all your secrets."

"I don't understand."

"Of course you don't," she huffed and rolled her dark eyes. "When I saw you and Nathan in the hospital the day you lost your baby, I instantly knew you didn't deserve him. Anyone could see how terrible you were for him."

"You what?" My tear ducts started to burn.

"You were so cold to him. He was trying to be the husband you needed him to be, and all you did was push him away. You wouldn't even let him touch you or hold his son."

I tilted my head. My eyes fixed on the woman who now possessed the body of the person I had known as Evelyn. "You were at the hospital that day?"

"I was assigned to the patient you were in the same room with," she answered. "Jesus, you're so self-absorbed you don't even remember, do you? I bet I was only sitting ten feet away from you."

Tears started to stream down my cheeks. "My son had just died," I yelped. "I was a little preoccupied."

"That's just it, Liz. You're always preoccupied with yourself," she snapped in response. "Were you really that shocked when Nathan had to find solace in the arms of another woman?"

"Who the fuck are you?" I demanded as I searched my mind for any memory of her. We had been waiting to be moved to a private room. The emergency wing had a bed shortage, and I'd been placed in the same room with a young lady whom the nurse felt frequently compelled to apologize to me about. She was at least nine months pregnant, her belly far more swollen than my own had been. The way she was babbling, I'd assumed she was high on something. I never spoke to her. There was no reason I would have. I remember Nathan telling the nurse to do whatever she had to to get us a private room. I couldn't remember Evelyn, though, no matter how hard I tried.

"Who the fuck am I? Well, Liz, since you had your mother look into me, it seems you should know exactly who I am."

"I just wanted to understand who I was talking to," I defended my actions.

"Yeah, just like you were looking out for Nathan when you started spying on Alison. You always have an excuse, don't you? It's never your fault. Did you ever think that none of this would have ever happened if you had cared about anyone besides yourself for two seconds?"

"I don't understand." It felt like all the air was being sucked out of my lungs.

"Not that you would ever care about someone else long enough to find out, but that young woman you shared a room with that day suffered from schizophrenia. She'd gone off her meds because she was scared they would hurt the baby. I was there to evaluate her," Evelyn explained.

"But you said you met Nathan at a grief meeting."

"I did," she replied. "But I didn't say that was the first time I'd seen him."

My head was starting to throb, and the room had begun to sway. *Not now, brain. Don't you fucking bug out on me now.*

"Anyone who saw him on that day could see that all he wanted to do was take your pain away. You couldn't let him help you, though, could you? No, it didn't matter that he had also just been gutted. You had to show him what he felt was nothing in comparison to what you felt."

"You're wrong—"

She interrupted me. "I see people like you all the time."

"You're crazy."

"You had a perfect life and threw it all away, and you think I'm crazy?" She was angry now, and the look on her face frightened me. I considered calling out to the guards as I glanced in their direction. "Did you see the case in the news or something? Is that why you approached Nathan?" I pressed.

She laughed again, only this time it sounded much more sinister. "Oh my God, you have no idea what's going on here, do you?"

I shook my head. "Please, enlighten me," I growled.

"After that first night when I saw the two of you in the hospital, I couldn't get you out of my mind. I felt drawn to both of you. I decided it was because you needed my help," she explained. "I didn't understand how exactly at first, but you made it very clear."

I resisted the urge to reach across the table and wrap my fingers around her pale white neck, tightening my grip until I deprived her of all oxygen. Instead, I bit into my lip, forcing myself to stay quiet as she continued. "But then I realized it was your husband who needed me, not the two of you. After a few weeks, it was pretty obvious that your marriage was imploding."

"You were watching us?" I asked, not shielding the disgust from my voice.

She laughed. "Really? You're going to act like I somehow violated your lives in some way after what you did with Alison?"

I looked away from her and pressed my lips together as I willed myself not to scream. She wasn't wrong. She hadn't done anything I hadn't done myself, which only served to make me feel even worse about my behavior.

"I watched when the affair started," she revealed.

"What?" I clenched my fists into two tight balls at my side. Evelyn's once pretty face was twisted into some sort of demon, and all I could think was that I wanted to kill her. Maybe I was a killer after all.

"You know, he resisted Alison at first," she said with a satisfied tone. "I was there at lunch, sitting just one booth away on a lunch date when Alison told him she was attracted to him. He told her he was flattered but he was a happily married man. Don't feel bad. That woman knew exactly how to push his buttons. I don't think any man could have resisted her. Hell, she was more ruthless than you when it came to manipulation."

"I never manipulated Nathan," I snapped defensively.

"Yeah, you keep telling yourself that. Anyway, I have to say thank you so much for the cameras. Even I never thought of that one."

My whole body had started trembling. "What's that supposed to mean?"

"You don't think I was just following Nathan around, do you?" she asked as she looked me in the eyes with an icy glare. "I mean, for Christ's sake, when you made up your mind that bitch was going to die, it was tough keeping up with you. But I will admit, all the legwork you did made everything so much easier when the time came."

The night I went to Alison's house flooded my mind. Was I alone in the house? I had to have been. Did I remember seeing anyone outside? I'd looked around, but I got out of there so fast. I was worried Alison could get home at any moment, and I didn't want to be there. I asked the question that I'd already known the answer to. I needed to hear her say it. "When what time came?"

"My gut said you'd never go through with it," she said. "It goes back to the fact that everything you do is just for attention. You wanted Nathan to catch you planning that girl's murder and then beg for your forgiveness, and he'd tell you it was all his fault he drove you to such a state. God, you are so transparent."

"I did not!" My voice raised. I didn't care if a guard heard us. Alison's killer was sitting right across from me.

My skin was so hot I thought my blood might start to boil.

"Okay, I'm not here to help you with your issues, Liz, so tell yourself whatever you need to."

"Why are you here?"

"Well, I told you," she stated, motioning toward the papers in her grasp. "I plan to marry Nathan, but I needed you to help me do that. I mean, the man takes a bit of pushing, doesn't he? I told him marrying me was probably the easiest way for him to move on and leave all of that nasty business in the past, but he just couldn't file those fucking papers."

"You're not going to get away with this."

"Look around. Thanks to you, I already did." She laughed. "You know the funniest part?"

A shiver rolled down my spine as I listened to her speak.

"I was trying to figure out how I was going to get you and Alison out of my way when I saw you show up in her house with that knife." Evelyn shook her head as she clicked her tongue against the roof of her mouth. "You provided me with everything I needed. I didn't think you could be that stupid, but you really were. The night you went over there, I almost started to respect you. I thought maybe you were finally going to take some action and reclaim your man, but then no, sure enough, you did exactly what I always assumed you would."

"How did you know I was there?"

She smiled. "I rented the house just down the street from Alison. It made it much easier to keep an eye on them. Well, that is, until you installed the cameras. I mean fuck, that was some pretty twisted shit. Don't get me wrong, I appreciated it. It was pretty simple to patch into them. I had a front-row seat, thanks to you. I must say, I don't know how you watched some of that freaky shit they were up to."

"Shut up!" I screamed, and from the corner of my eye, I saw I'd gained the attention of one of the guards.

"Oh, did I strike a nerve?"

"You're not going to get away with this!"

"Yeah, yeah, you said that. I saw it on the cameras when you got there that night. When you removed them but left before Alison got home, I knew you were never going to do what needed to be done. Honestly, if you had, I might have let you have Nathan. But in the end, you showed me you didn't deserve him."

"You followed me," I muttered.

"Now you're catching on. That's when I saw you toss the bag. What if a kid had found that? You never were mother material, were you?"

I looked over at the guard again, trying to decide what I could yell to cause them to detain Evelyn.

"What? Thinking of trying to tell them?" she asked as she watched my eyes. "Go ahead. Nobody's going to believe you. You'll look like a jealous ex who is trying to stop your husband from moving on. I mean, hell, a jury convicted you of killing his last girlfriend, so it's not too far-fetched that you would lie about the next one. There is nothing that links me to him before the murder. Nothing that would help your story make sense."

"Fine, then I'll tell him."

"Nathan?" She laughed as she said his name. "He won't believe you either. He hates you."

"I guess we'll see."

"Don't you get it? He won't want to believe you because I am giving him the thing you never could."

"What are you talking about?"

Her eyes moved down as she touched her stomach. "I'm pregnant." When I heard the words, the thumping inside my head started to pound louder, and I felt the acid from my stomach as it began to climb up my throat.

"You're lying," I spat the words in disbelief.

She raised three fingers as if she were taking an oath. "Honest to God, I'm right around three months now."

I had been angry with Alison. I thought I wanted her dead, but it was nothing like the rage and fury I'd felt at that moment as I looked across the table at Evelyn Powell's smug expression. "Nathan is so excited. He'll be pretty miffed when he finds out I came back here to talk to you again, but when he sees you signed the papers, well, I just know he will be so ecstatic for us to get our family started."

"He'll see through you."

She mocked my words in a high-pitched whine. "Yeah, I doubt it. I'm the one who's pregnant with his baby."

"You bitch."

She frowned. "You're so predictable. It's boring now."

"Why tell me all this?"

"Are you kidding? Do you know how patient I had to be? I had to wait for every single thing to fall into place. Unlike you. You always acted on impulse." She tilted her head. "But that's not the type of person Nathan needs in his life. If he's going to reach his full potential, he will need someone at his side who will add to him. I would do anything to help Nathan, unlike you. You and Alison, all the two of you ever cared about was what Nathan could do for you."

"How'd you do it?" I asked. My eyes started to fill with tears again.

"How did I do what?"

"How did you make him fall in love with you?"

She thought over the question and then stood. I started to panic as I realized she was about to leave. She grinned as she took one step back from the table. "You don't get to know everything."

"He's going to figure this out," I stated through gritted teeth as I tried to decide if I could leap across the table and squeeze the life out of her before the guards pulled me off.

She shook her head and leaned in a bit closer to me. "That's what you don't understand about men, Liz. He doesn't want to figure it out. I'm the woman who was there for him at his lowest after his wife betrayed him and murdered his pregnant girlfriend. I'm the woman who is finally giving him the family he always wanted."

"You fucking cunt," I growled under my breath as I gripped the edge of the table and glared up at her.

"You should be thanking me," she added before she turned to walk away.

"You're sick!"

She started to walk away and pulled her lips into a frown. She glanced at the guard as she approached and shook her head. "So sad," she whispered in the direction of the guard.

"Fuck you!" I shouted as I leaped from my seat and raced toward Evelyn. I knew there was no way I would ever reach her, but if by the off chance a guard took a moment to notice, maybe I had just enough time to slam her head against the glass before one of the guards restrained me.

"You need help. I hope you finally get it in here." I heard Evelyn say just as a loud cracking noise let loose in my head, and I felt all the air deflate out of my lungs. I skidded back and fell to the floor with a thud. Within seconds, I felt one of the guard's weight across my legs as she secured my hands behind my back with a zip tie. She issued me a warning, but I wasn't listening. I strained upward and watched as Evelyn walked out of the door of the visitation room.

I started screaming frantically. I begged them to stop her. I tried to tell them she was the real killer and that I was innocent. Just as Evelyn had predicted, though, they didn't listen. Or maybe, it was more that they didn't care. It wasn't their job to figure out who was guilty and who was innocent. The jury had already decided that.

They dragged me to the infirmary while I fought them every step of the way—the halls blurred as I passed in and out of consciousness. When I awoke, once again strapped to the bed, Dr. Weber was taking my vitals.

I tried to tell her what I'd just discovered. She encouraged me to calm down and take a deep breath. She explained I'd blacked out again.

I had started to scream at some point, desperate for

someone to listen and hear that I shouldn't be here. The doctor inserted a needle into my arm and told me everything would be okay in a soothing voice. It wasn't okay. I couldn't make any of them see that nothing would ever be okay because this woman had stolen my entire life.

Instead, I fell silent under the power of the sedation, destined to sit in prison, just as Dr. Evelyn Powell had planned. I thought of her carrying those papers I had signed in her hands as she drove home. To their home. Eager to deliver the news that they were free of me at last.

I stared up at the ceiling, my limbs going numb as I started to laugh. In trying to take back my husband from Alison, I'd opened him up to an even scarier predator. Evelyn would marry Nathan, and I would rot in here, seen as a woman gone mad with jealousy.

∼

EPILOGUE

"Lauren, I'm so glad you're here." Tears threatened to break free as soon as I entered the room.

"I would have been here sooner, but apparently, you were put on another psych hold? What is going on with you, Liz?" my lawyer asked, and I could see she was concerned by the way she looked at me.

"I know who the killer is." The words slipped out in a whisper. I was scared to say them. So scared she wouldn't believe me.

A scowl appeared on Lauren's face.

"I'm not lying. She confessed to me."

She pulled her lips in tightly and hesitated to speak for a moment. "Who confessed to you?"

"Nathan's new fiancée is a doctor at Mass General, and she's been coming here to see me to get me to sign divorce papers."

"That seems like a bad idea to take those visits, Liz. I would recommend against it."

"Yeah, I could have used that advice a few months ago, but it's a little late now." I shook my head as I continued. "She's crazy! She told me that I didn't deserve Nathan and that she killed Alison and pinned it on me."

"Wait." Lauren lifted a hand. "She told you this?"

"Yes! Can you order her DNA?" I answered.

Lauren thought about my question before she shook her head. "What's her name?"

"Dr. Evelyn Powell."

Lauren sighed.

"What's wrong?" I asked, my heart pounding wildly in my chest.

"I don't know what game this woman is playing, but I don't think she's the one who killed Alison," Lauren explained.

"No, she told me!"

"I understand what she told you, Liz, but the federal database came back with a match on the other DNA that was found at the crime scene."

"What?" I gasped. "So we've got her."

"That's just it. It belonged to a woman from Georgia who went missing from a psych hospital. Her name was Patty Dane."

I shook my head in confusion. "Who the hell is Patty Dane?"

"I have our private investigator looking into it," Lauren started. "But the important part is this is the evidence we needed to get you a new trial."

"No, it doesn't make sense. Evelyn said she killed Alison," I insisted.

Lauren chuffed. "Who cares? This is the best possible

outcome for you. This Patty woman had been locked up for stalking some guy she worked with. Do you even understand the doubt I can create with that DNA being on the scene?"

My brow furrowed as I tried to make sense of what Lauren was telling me. "I don't understand. This Patty woman went missing? Could she be working with Evelyn?"

"Maybe. I'm waiting on details from our investigator, but apparently, from what I've been told so far, she walked right out the front door of the hospital she was at a few years ago, and nobody has seen her since."

Lauren reached across the table and gripped my hand. "Liz, when I'm done with your case, you're going home."

I looked at my lawyer and smiled. "Thank you." I managed at last, as my eyes grew wet. I didn't know who this woman from Georgia was, but I was sure Evelyn had stolen my life. The moment I got out of here, I was coming for her.

∼

ACKNOWLEDGMENTS

To my readers: I wouldn't be able to do what I do without your desire to read my books. Thank you from the bottom of my heart.

Thank you to my three kids, Zoe, Brayden, and Penelope, you all make me proud every single day and I feel both lucky and loved being your mom.

Thank you to Josh. You turn my doubts into motivation on a weekly basis. I am not the easiest to live with, especially when I have deadlines. Your loyalty is fierce and I am thankful it's mine. I love you always.

ABOUT THE AUTHOR

Wendy Owens, was raised in the small college town of Oxford, Ohio. Wendy happily spends her days writing—her loving dachshund, Piper Von Snitzel, curled up at her feet along side her sister, a Labrador mix, River Song. When she's not writing, she can be found spending time with her true love, her tech geek husband and their three amazing kids.

To follow everything current with Wendy Owens' Books:
https://signup.wendyowensbooks.com/

ALSO BY WENDY OWENS

Find links to all of Wendy's Books at
wendyowensbooks.com/books/

PSYCHOLOGICAL THRILLER

My Husband's Fiancée

YA ROMANCE

Wash Me Away

YA PARANORMAL (clean)

Sacred Bloodlines

Unhallowed Curse

The Shield Prophecy

The Lost Years

The Guardians Crown

CONTEMPORARY ROMANCE (adult)

Stubborn Love

Only In Dreams

The Luckiest

Do Anything

It Matters to Me

NA URBAN FANTASY

Burning Destiny

Blazing Moon

COZY MYSTERIES

Jack Be Nimble, Jack Be Dead

O Deadly Night

Roses Are Red, Violet is Dead

∽

Made in the USA
Middletown, DE
03 December 2021